Old Friends

Old

A NOVEL

Friends

STEPHEN DIXON

MELVILLE HOUSE PUBLISHING
HOBOKEN, NEW JERSEY

Book design by David Konopka

Melville House Publishing
P.O. Box 3278
Hoboken NJ 07030

mhpbooks.com

ISBN: 0-9749609-2-6

First edition

Library of Congress Cataloging-in-Publication Data

Dixon, Stephen, 1936-
   Old friends : a novel / Stephen Dixon.-- 1st ed.
       p. cm.
   ISBN 0-9749609-2-6
   I. Title.
   PS3554.I92O44 2004
   813'.54--dc22

                              2004016101

TO MY FRIENDS
HENRY H. ROTH AND DAVID EVANIER

Katya said "If you're going to stay here for more than a few days while I'm at work, it's probably a good idea to have someone else in the area to talk to occasionally. I know another writer nearby who's dying for literary company, his son, a student of mine, says. Lives just two miles from here. He doesn't drive or ride a bike so you'll have to get to his house on my bike or by walking or jogging there if it's not too rainy or cold. That is, if you two hit it off, which I feel confident you will."

Irv had started seeing Katya the month before. They'd met in a bookstore, talked about a book she was examining to see if she wanted to teach it to her high school students, she took his phone number rather than give him hers and surprised him by calling a few hours later. He had an apartment in New York, she rented a small house in a town in Rockland County, about twenty miles from him. He usually went up to see her by bus but sometimes she came down in her car, parked on his block, did some chores with or without him or they went to a movie or play or museum and then drove to her house and he'd return to the city by bus the next day or two. But he'd been laid off from his salesman's job at a department store and started spending more time at her house. This afternoon around five, moments after she came through the door, he said "Boy, am I glad to see you. Your kid's out till six, you don't ever seem to get back from school till dark, there wasn't a single phone call or bird peep or hawk squawk from outdoors, so for a while I was talking to myself or the walls. Want to hear what I had to say?" and she said "This is what I was afraid would happen if you were alone here too long, but I think I have the solution."

"This fellow's writing life is so much like yours," she said, "it's practically uncanny. He's been writing for about fifteen years—" and he said "I've been doing it for around twelve." "Twelve, fifteen, he's a little older than you, but you get my point. There's more, though. Like you he's published lots of stories in little magazines," and he said "I've only had about eight. Yes," counting them in his head, "eight exactly, but that's both little and big." "To me that's a lot. He's said the majority of his have been in very small obscure magazines but that he once had one in *Esquire* when he was first starting out, and another a few years ago in *New American Review*. I liked that magazine, or paperback—what would you call it, and why'd it fold?" and he said "It's come back. Now it's the

American Review. I've a story in one of the next three issues."
"See? One more thing in common. But no *Esquire*, though you
did say you had two in *Playboy*," and he said "In my early
heyday and when it was a more literary magazine, and one in
Harper's, soon after that." "So you have two more big magazine
publications than he does but he's got about forty little magazines over you. But never a book published, either of you,
though he's said he's tried very hard with story collections and
novels and several times got quite close." "Me too," Irv said.
"Collections, novels, very hard, never close. But really, I'm
fine as is. My longing for you during the day or just the sound
of company in general was a temporary anomaly, and I'm not
good at blind dates. From now on I'll do what I said I would
while you're at work: write all day, take long walks if
I need distraction. Or just read and go to the library and, if I
feel like it—and why not? I've just come off a job where
I worked my tail off for a year—nap." "No, you're bound to
end up being a drag on me, while there'll be less chance of it
if you chat with Leonard from time to time. He also doesn't
have a job, though unlike you he hasn't had one since he delivered flowers when he was fifteen," and he said "Okay, I'll take
the first step: Leonard what?" and when she told him, "Hey,
I've seen his stuff around for years. We in fact were in the same
little magazine once. He's pretty good, or at least a heck of
a lot better than most writers in them. Family comedies or
dramas usually, most with a sensitive young-son narrator.

I also recall a very solid baseball story, which is hard to do because they can so easily become sentimental and predictable and the hero such a dumb bore. Lots of Jewish life and lore in his work, even the baseball one. He must have had an extensive religious education, maybe even a yeshiva or comparable Hebrew high school and a year on an Orthodox kibbutz, and I bet his family kept kosher but that he gave all that up. Father usually gentle and henpecked and keeping a woman for years and mother always a vivid loud character or nuts and son an only child and, because of his parents, ripe for psychotherapy. All traditionally written, as if no tricks was part of his aesthetic credo, but with humor, not very deep emotionally and certainly smoothly done and unpretentious—never a big word or heady thought—and accessible and clear. Though occasionally clumsy phrasing and scene-setting and situation solving, as if he rushed through it because he was so eager to get to the next story, or heavy rewriting to work out the inconsistencies and sloppiness was too much like punishment or a tedious grind. Lots of good dialogue, I remember. From what I've read of him, that's his forte and what comes most naturally to him, and description and such much less so and what he probably had to work hard on years back to get the little facility he now has with it, so I'm sure he's also written plays but eschews poetry both to read and write."

Katya said "You'd get a kick and maybe even a story out of how I got to meet Leonard and Suzanne, his wife. Want to hear it?" and he said "Go ahead, but wait'll I get my pad and pen."

"Manfred, their only child, is the smartest and my favorite student in my English honors-class, and for months insisted I meet his folks. They're wild and eccentric, he said—Suzanne wild and both of them eccentric, and because I have the same qualities and a comparable sense of humor, he's sure they'll love me. He meant that as a compliment, for he's also complained to me how stiff, impersonal and just plain dumb, depressed and incompetent most of the other teachers are. So one day right before lunch period he said why don't we drive to his house to see his dad? He was sure he'd be home, since Leonard holes up there writing from nine to three except for time-outs to walk Farrah, their dog, and lumber to the post office once a week to weigh and mail manuscripts to magazines. I went with him in his car even though I knew I wasn't supposed to. But at the time I was lonely for adult company in town—just Lily and me and her goldfinch in our compact house—and I also thought Leonard could be a hot line to other interesting and intelligent men in the area. It turned out that the few male friends he'd made in his fifteen years there were happily married or dour confirmed bachelors like some of the teachers I taught with and not all that pals-y with him, and Suzanne only knew single or divorced women on the prowl themselves for interesting, intelligent men. Anyway, I liked them both but felt that Suzanne saw me as a threat to her with Leonard—it was apparent he had a roaming eye though I doubted he acted on it—so I haven't had that much to do with them, but introducing you to him should be safe." Irv said "Okay, because why am I fighting it, and unlike with most writers I can actually say nice things about his work and mean it. You can tell from his work he's not in it for the glory or dough but is a real writer, meaning he loves doing it and is driven crazy when he can't get to his typewriter every day. How do I know and what's probably also so that he's never blocked but always has a story to write? It's just a feeling, just as I can tell from a writer's work that he doesn't like the act of writing. It's also possible, since he seems pretty prolific too, that we can give each other tips how to get our stuff out more—you know, editors and agents I might know or have heard of and he might not and the reverse."

She called Leonard, said after "He said great, come over around five, and he thinks he once read a fiction of yours in a little magazine. And though he didn't know if it was a story or part of a novel, since it didn't have the completion he expects in a story, or really any ending at all, it wasn't half bad and he wants to ask you if he'd possibly missed something in it. Did you ever publish a piece where a man slams his fist through a door because he's so upset when his girlfriend dumps him?" and he said "Yes, and another with a fiancée when she breaks off the engagement a week before the wedding, but in that one it's a door, window, bathroom partition and the back of a chair." They went that night and were offered herbal tea, juice or soda. Irv said "Excuse me for my crassness, but is there anything harder to drink in this house? If not, fine, but I was thinking maybe Katya told you I was a teetotaler or a belligerent drunk, for I could go for a shot of something in a glass of ice or a wine or beer." "We never have any alcohol around," Suzanne said. "Leonard can't stand the taste of it and half a glass of anything alcoholic puts me right to sleep. Guests come to dinner—this visit isn't, though feel free, if you like, to join us at the table later while we eat—I tell them to bring and drink their own booze, we'll provide the swizzle sticks if they need and some very fine glassware." Good God, Irv thought, what pills, and with nothing to drink how's he going to tolerate them for even this short stay? But after half an hour of talk and showing him around the house—she; Leonard never got out of his big easy chair once he'd sat in it or took his feet off the ottoman—he hit it off with them both. Leonard: lots of funny jokes, witty asides, entertaining anecdotes, interesting and informative comments on books and writers, especially his two favorites whom he reads a little of every day and has been doing so for twenty years: Babel and Chekhov. Suzanne had no interest in fiction, least of all Leonard's, she said, "since he tells me in detail scene by scene while he's writing his stories and then what he did in each revision, till I feel I've not only read but also written them." She was a terrific artist: woodcuts, engravings, linoleum-block prints. Her work was on the walls: all mythological themes from a variety of cultures: birds of prey devouring men's livers, testicles and eyes; women being laid or raped by dolphins, elephants and bulls; breasts—ten of them on one woman's chest—feeding different kinds of animals at once; newborn humans and monkeys, their umbilical cords still attached, tumbling together out of a cornucopian cunt. She was smart about art and how to teach it but sort of scatterbrained about other things. Kept calling Irv the name of Katya's former husband whom she'd met once. Started leading him up a short staircase and then stopped and said "My goodness, what am I doing? Half these steps are rotted, so they now only lead to a boarded-up door. Let's use the back route." Said to him "Can I get you a peppermint tea?" and he thought what the hell, why not? Something warm to hold and press to his cheek in this house made cold by a number of broken window panes she said they'd been meaning to replace since summer. And his mouth was dry from a potato chip–pretzel stick combination she'd put out, so he said "Thanks," and she went into the kitchen and came back fifteen minutes later and sat down and then said "Oh my gosh, I forgot to make you tea. I got lost doing some-thing else in the kitchen, but I forget what," and went back to get him the tea and didn't return. "She's preparing an elaborate dinner," Katya said when she led Irv to the bathroom upstairs and he asked where Suzanne was, "and wants us to stay to help eat it." "Good, I'm enjoying myself and am hungry and the food smells great. But if we're staying, let me get a bottle of wine," and she said that was unnecessary, one meal he could do without it, and he said "But it's a better meal with, and I want to warm myself in your car," and drove a few miles to the nearest open liquor store. Suzanne tried starting a fire in the fireplace after dinner and said to Leonard "I thank you for your one physical effort of the week other than your incessant typewriter banging, which I don't find much to be thankful for when I'm home except that it keeps you out of my hair. But if you are going to collect loose wood from around the house, how can you be so unaware? It's all wet and green." "Wood's wood," Leonard said. "If the bottom layer, laid across a bed of shredded-up paper, is thin enough—twigs I'm talking about here—the fire will eventually start. And once it really gets going, the rest of the wet wood you throw on—branches of increasing size till you end up with actual split logs which we don't have, since they don't fall from our trees—will dry and eventually catch fire, just as the twigs did from the burning paper. I was an Eagle scout of the highest order—I soared—and earned fifty merit badges and a huge neurosis to show for it, which helped make me the lazy bum I am today, and used to start fires with just the sun's rays through a piece of broken glass." Irv volunteered to help and got a little fire going by using lots of paper and sorting out the driest twigs and blowing on it for about fifteen minutes, and Suzanne said to him "Now that's my idea of a male *mensch*. Worked for a living till he was bounced, even if it was a lousy low-paying job, while also finding time to fuss with his creative spirit, and around the house doesn't just talk but pitches in." "Oh, please," Irv said. "I just bungle on from day to day and, as far as the creative crap goes, plug away trying to make something out of nothing and to keep out of my own hair," and Leonard said "No, she's right, listen to her, and no silly humility. You're doing good, though you can also see who she's not too insidiously carping about, but that's all right. Though you did prove my point about starting fires with wood in any condition. Although the blowing part, which I didn't think necessary—a second bed of slightly larger twigs, wet or dry, would have done it—could have a lasting damaging effect on your lungs because of all the smoke you sucked in." Driving back to Katya's, Irv said "I liked her at first, or let's say soon after I didn't much care for her, but after a whole evening of her I didn't know how he could take that shit from her or why she was trying so hard to humiliate him in front of us," and she said "Why Suzanne does it? To let off steam, because I'm sure nothing works on him when she tells him when they're alone. And as for his reason? He has a small stipend every month from his father, she told me. But she's the main breadwinner, handyman and child rearer—he was only good for teaching Manfred how to play baseball—so he has to put up with it if he wants to continue sitting on his ass writing all day. I like Leonard for all the reasons I already told you. Especially that he speaks his mind about things when it means something—that sort of flaky wood-burning routine was either out of character or had a hidden meaning that eluded me but she knew what it meant—and is frank, open and honest about himself without it seeming like an unasked-for confession. That said, if I were Suzanne—and she's loaded with talent and energy and still quite pretty and young enough to attract some good men—I would have told him long ago to shape up and find a job or get the hell out and don't forget to take all your manuscripts."

He saw Leonard a lot the next three years whenever he stayed at Katya's and then in New York after he and Katya got an apartment there—Leonard would take the bus in and they'd have lunch, go for long walks and browse in bookstores—and then after Katya broke up with him. He'd wanted to marry her and have a child. She needed someone more reliable, she said; he barely made enough to support a single frugal man skimpily and she also wanted to see what her value was on the social marketplace, as she put it, and knew he'd hate her dating other men and probably sleeping with some of them while she was still living with him. He'd also probably object to her sleeping with other men while she was dating and no doubt sleeping with him, which was why she wanted it to be a complete break. And let's face it, she said, he's had a good run for his money with her. Among other things, fairly steady companionship and sex; for the last eighteen months, a bright spacious apartment in New York which he paid less than half the rent for, since her daughter also lived with them; introducing him to what turned out to be his best male friend or certainly the one he has most in common with; and the last four and a half years the equiv- alent of two story collections and now the first hundred pages of the many ups and downs and intermittent harmonious interludes of their relationship. That was another thing that contributed to her wanting to split up with him, she said. She was tired of having almost everything she did, and many of the extemporaneous things she said, chronicled in his work. Like her flossing her teeth after each meal and before sleep; her quick sponge baths when she was too in a rush to take a shower; reading the arts section of the *Times* on the toilet lots of mornings (why do so many things he writes about her have to take place in the bathroom, she said); her appendectomy scar a few times, once on the wrong side of her body; her large feet and relatively short height and the coital position she disliked most; getting pregnant by him and he wanting her to have the baby and she being forced to start off to the abortion clinic alone; her mother dying and her father periodically being institutionalized and her daughter's first period and signs of breast development, which if she ever read the story would embarrass her; even her ex-husband who isn't the conniving and affected bad egg he portrayed him as or not as much. She was in fact doing him a service by cutting him loose and refusing to see and possibly sleep with again, she said. She felt he'd run out of material with her other than for this speech of hers and their final irrevocable breakup and his going back to his crummy apartment and thinking about her if that was what he was going to do, so it'd only be repeats of what he'd already written about her and published the last three to four years.

Leonard didn't drink any kind of coffee and the only tea he drank had to be uncaffeinated. He'd never smoked, not even a single puff of anything. Never taken a hallucinogen or drug like that of any kind; although he might have eaten a couple of pot cookies at a party by mistake, but if he did, and he was told he had, it had no effect. He didn't have a driver's license and had never applied for one and when he was a kid he had never, he said, wanted to drive or own a bike or car. "I figured there'd always be public transportation where I lived, and which I prefer because of the exotic types you find on it and interesting conversations you overhear, and that when I got married my wife and later on my kid would drive a car." He'd never been to Europe, never wanted to leave the country. "As my dad liked to say, 'Everything is here so why go there and have to pay double for it?' That's part of the reason: dough. Mostly, though, I wouldn't like leaving my typewriter behind or lugging it around with me, and I don't like sleeping in hotel beds a thousand guys have jacked off in." The only traveling he'd done had been to a few Northeast states when he went to sleepaway camp for the summer, but not Maine, New Hampshire or Vermont, and once for a week when he was a boy and his mother and he stayed with an uncle and aunt in Philadelphia. "I've good memories of that city, thought one day I might go back to it and then continue on to D.C., but never have." He'd never been to a farm but saw a few from the bus when he was driven to summer camp. He was afraid of all animals but small songbirds and most dogs and cats. He'd been to one opera and ballet in his life—"And not just one because I like to try something at least once. If I don't think I'll like something, I try to stay completely away"—and a couple of concerts and a few Off-Broadway and Broadway plays, one of those because a rep company was interested in turning a few of his interrelated stories into a full-length play and he wanted to see it in action. "Nothing happened with my stories or in the play I saw. The other plays and musicals I went to I either slept through or sat there thinking about my own writing but nothing in connection to what was on stage." Cultural events like operas and serious music concerts, he said, he didn't appreciate or understand, and as for the opera he couldn't make out the language even when it was sung or spoken slowly in English. "And they're always too loud and long, though the one piano recital I was also dragged to over my own dead body was so soft at times that I couldn't hear, and we were sitting up front. I did like the ballet at the City Center because of the ballerinas and their firm fannies and legs, but what the dancing was trying to say drew a blank from me." He liked movies, he said, and going to them, though the minute they got artsy or dark they turned him off. Museums it was true he should go to more because of Suzanne, but she wouldn't go to one with him because of the cracks he always made about the work on the walls and floors—"I can't help it; what she does is about the only kind I like, but that didn't score any points with her since she's right when she says I know nothing about the field"—and anyway he could only be in one for a max of twenty minutes before his feet got tired and his stomach hurt. Fiction was the only art form he liked and was familiar enough with to talk about with any sense, he said. "All I want to do in my life is read and write, and so far I've been fairly successful at it, not in my writing as a money-making career or even as an art form, but in being able to do it almost anytime I want." He didn't like reading poetry or literary criticism or really anything about literature except an occasional book review and a fiction writer's preface to his reissued novel or big volume of selected stories, because he usually found them slow-going and didn't know what the poet or critic meant. "It's possible if I put my mind to it I'd eventually figure out what they were saying but that would involve more time than I'd want to take away from the reading I like to do and the thinking, which isn't great but can be time-consuming, that goes into my own writing." He has read biographies, but only of Kafka and Chekhov and one of Chekhov's wife, and a long one of Hemingway that he never finished. The only magazines he read were little literary ones for their short stories and sometimes an interview with a fiction writer he liked. He didn't read newspapers except the sports section during baseball season. Didn't watch TV either except baseball. "My enjoyment of that sport isn't because of its scientific and mathematical makeup, since I'm not interested in anything related to science and math either. Baseball's the only activity other than reading and writing I was good at and liked to do as a boy. So, being a very limited person and for the last twenty-five years not being especially open to doing anything new except in my writing, it probably carried through." Whenever he wanted money, he'd ask Suzanne for cash. The only form of identification he had was a Social Security card, which he had to get when he got a job when he was fifteen. He'd been told that if he did have a checking account or one jointly shared with his wife, he wouldn't be able to use that card as ID to cash a check. He didn't have a passport or voter's registration card and had never voted. He got no junk mail, he said, because he didn't vote or have a driver's license or insurance policy or credit card or savings or checking account and was a member of no organization and had never ordered anything by mail or subscribed to a magazine and his name wasn't listed in the phone book—only Suzanne's—so he was on no list. He had changed a few light bulbs in the house over the years and jiggled the lever on a toilet tank to stop the water from running and carpetswept the living room rug and mowed the lawn with a push mower, but no home repair or chores more complicated than that. They were given a microwave by her parents but he didn't know how to operate it and didn't want to learn. He was able to boil water on the gas stove and toast bread and open cans with a can opener and make chocolate milk and hot chocolate if he was using water. He had never cooked his son dinner. When Manfred was younger—"Now he sometimes makes dinner for us, and he's a pretty good cook, though I'll eat anything set before me"—and Leonard had to give him dinner because Suzanne was out, she prepared it beforehand and he either warmed it on the stove—he'd never turned the oven on or used it ("I'm afraid I'll gas us or blow up the house")—or served it cold with some bread he'd butter and milk he'd pour. He had also never made a more complicated lunch for Manfred than a peanut butter and jelly sandwich— "Adding the jelly was a major kitchen advancement for me, and I even after a while figured out which one to smear on the bread first"—and sliced carrots and celery sticks—"Another of my food accomplishments, slicing carrots crosswise or straight up and down and washing celery and lettuce." He'd never learned to swim. Never been on ice or roller skates and hadn't been on a bike in thirty years. "I got into a bad accident on one when I was ten. I didn't get hurt but the bike did—front totally smashed when a bus ran over it, and that was all my folks needed to stop me from riding one again. Instead of taking the 'sooner you get back on, quicker you'll forget the trauma of nearly getting killed,' they wouldn't buy or rent me another one. 'You get one bike in your life before you have to pay for your own,' they said—remember, I was only ten, five years away from getting my one and only job—'because you know what those damn things cost? As for renting, you'll just inherit someone else's problems, and the chain will fall off before you're three feet out of the store.'" He once liked jazz, he said, and would put one of his records on every so often if their record player wasn't broken. "We could buy a new one but then I don't think it'd be worth it for the few times a year I might play it, and Suzanne thinks music's a big waste of time. I'd use Manfred's in his room, but the kid, knowing how I tend to break simple things I touch—my eyeglasses frame has a life span of about two weeks before I sit on it—won't let me go near it or his baseball bat and glove." He once said "Wait, in relation to what we were talking about some time ago?—there is something else I read besides fiction and a few literary bios and short prefaces, and that's letters by writers, but only Chekhov's and Flaubert's. Between them, those two guys in their letters have said everything there is about the writing process and habit." As a boy he never had many friends, he said. "Make that, I only had a few and rarely more than one at a time and never that one for very long, and half of them, because I was from early on interested in them in a sort of sexy way, were girls. Main reason my friendships didn't last too long, other than for if the girls got wise to me trying to cop a feel every now and then, was that I got a very small allowance, and some weeks, for behavior I'm sure my parents intentionally misinterpreted as bad so they could save on the quarter or fifty cents, nothing. This meant I couldn't do the things my friends liked to after school and on Sundays—getting a snack or chipping in for a comic book or even going to a movie. Saturdays, of course, I had to spend hanging around the house doing nothing or trying to cop a feel from girls at *shul*." Also, he said, his friends didn't like coming over to his place because of his parents, "who wouldn't part with a slice of stale bread they could make into toast if the kid was hungry. And if he said he was thirsty, he got milky tap water, while at their homes I got apple juice or milk and sometimes even a bottle of soda to share with my friend. My mother... crazy, right?—called these kids 'spies from the outside' who would tell lies about what went on in our home that would get us kicked out of the building and maybe my parents thrown in jail for communicating with the devil or the country's foreign enemies and me dumped into a place for temporarily orphaned boys and end up in a foster home where the adults there beat and starve me. In other words, she gave off something these kids in two minutes flat took to be 'I'm not happy with your injecting yourself into our home and staying longer than I expected or want you to.' My father, to keep the peace, went along with almost everything she fantasized or said, and would agree with her that my new friend at the time would teach me things they didn't want me to know, like listening to afternoon radio serials like *Sergeant Tennessee* and playing with marbles in the street and eating sweets." One time, Leonard said, he asked his parents if he could have a birthday party at home like other kids—he was about eight or nine. "They said 'Why, who would you invite? You have no friends.' And I said 'Bernie,' a kid on my block who was my present best friend, though I knew I wasn't his, and they said 'A party for only two? Since when is that done?

Also since when are you and Bernie such buddy-buddies, since we never see him here?' So I said 'I can also invite kids in my class I don't know that good but I know would come. Because no kid my age would turn down a birthday party where there'd be ice cream and soda and layer cake and things, and that way I could even make more friends than just Bernie.' They said 'What, so a half-dozen or more foul-mouthed brats with dirt under their fingernails and in their ears can come here and steal everything that isn't nailed down and eat us out of house and home? No. When the big event comes we'll sing that silly little Happy Birthday ditty at dinner and give you a hug and present. We haven't bought you one yet but we will,' they said, 'and that'll be more than enough celebrating for you for one year.' But they never bought me a birthday present or sang the song ever and the hugs were usually when my mother was depressed and needed one from me, and I never once had a birthday party. They said they gave me one when I was one or two, but of course I don't remember and think they were fibbing. 'Who came to it?' I said around that same time I asked for a party, and they said 'Cousins, uncles, aunts, the boy your age from the top floor who moved out with his family soon after—don't worry, you had nothing to do with their leaving.' And the only birthday party I remember being invited to as a kid I couldn't bring a present to, since my parents wouldn't buy one. 'More junk people don't need,' they said, 'so the boy's parents will be grateful to you for not bringing anything.'"

Leonard had a brother who died six years before he was born. "So you can say I never had a brother and, knowing my folks, never would've been born if he hadn't died. That's what they liked to hint when they thought I'd been bad, my mother always much more than my dad." There was a big framed tinted photograph of his brother above the fake fireplace in the living room, he said, taken by a professional kid photographer a few months before he died. "Since they didn't know he was ill then, I can't believe they'd put out the dough for it. Maybe it was a trade, one photo with blue skies and a Swiss mountain range behind the subject, for a gross box of my father's shoelaces in assorted sizes—that's what he manufactured for forty years in a little cement building in Brooklyn. Or maybe they were different then, and Semel's death—well, of course it did; I got to grant them that—changed them. It probably even made my mother crazy. He was such a handsome boy and with the sweetest disposition a child could hope to have, they said, and all this comes out in the photo—the good looks and sweet smile. These were also things they never thought I had, since they never once in my life said a nice thing to me about the way I looked and behaved. With me it was always 'Stand straight, your posture's lousy; you look like an old man already, and comb your hair. Stop drooling; you got spit running down both sides of your mouth; you want to be a slob, do it in private. Wash your hands again; they might look clean, but the way you take care of yourself, they're probably not, and show better manners at the table. Pick up your feet and don't move your arms back and forth when you walk; you look like a gorilla. Be obedient,' I heard a million times; 'listen to us, pay attention, don't turn your eyes away, always do what we say. Don't go near an open window above the first floor. Never cross the street by yourself'—even when I was eleven or twelve. All right, they were being extra protective of me because of Semel, but they never told me any of these things without also saying something like 'Remember, if you do get hit by a car, we warned you.' And this, I swear, once: 'You lose a leg walking between subway cars and falling off, don't come crying to us.' And about my brains: 'Good, you listened to us; now you're being smart for a change.' If I got a good report card, and I always did very well in school without much effort, they'd say 'This is okay, but it's what you should be getting; anything less we don't expect and won't accept. Your brother, he was so smart; first in his first-grade class for the whole school, and if they had a way to find out, probably in all of Brooklyn. His teachers said he had the makings of a science and math genius. He could have helped you with your homework what you don't know and boosted your grades even more, but what can you do? You just, like us, have to live without him and with the "oh-what-could-have-been",' and then my mother would break down and say 'Come here, come here,' and when I wouldn't, she'd grab me and hug me till my chest hurt and I'd say, if I was able to speak, 'Please, Mom, I need air.'" When he was ten, Leonard said, he took down Semel's photograph and hid it, and when they didn't seem to notice it gone after a week, put it back. "I was going to say when they asked me where it was: 'I don't know; God must have taken it if you didn't, so speak to Him.' I knew I'd get a good slap for that and several more before I was forced to admit I took it and gave it back. I never knew what to make of their not noticing it gone. The photo had been in the middle of the most prominent wall and now there was just empty space and at least twice a week, it seemed, I used to catch them, especially my mother, looking at Semel for a few seconds." Leonard had the same portable manual typewriter for about twenty years and never once got it cleaned or repaired. Two of the keys were missing. "Thankfully not important ones, which I can't explain, since you'd think the 'e,' 'i' and 'o' would go first. Suzanne and now Manfred changed the ribbon for him twice a year. "I wait till it gets so ragged that it starts catching in those tiny metal guide-things it goes through where the keys hit the roller." He said he used to try changing it himself but always got the ribbon twisted upside down and could never straighten it out. He'd never had a tan in his life, he said. "I wasn't allowed out in the summer sun without these goony pants down past my knees and a long-sleeved shirt and wide-brimmed straw hat, and usually not even near the shore with all those clothes on because of the sun's reflection off the water. My skin got so pale and soft from this that when I finally got away from my parents' physical clutches I was afraid if I went around in only a bathing suit and tank top, I'd burn in the sun." Suzanne and Manfred took month-long summer vacations together in places like Cape Cod and the Hamptons and he always stayed home with the dog and mainly wrote. "I hate sand, which is either deathly dry and too hot for your feet or soggy and tough to walk on, and if I don't have a tree hanging over my house, which you mostly can't at a beach, I feel suffocated and exposed." When they were gone he lived on simple sandwiches and canned soup or ate at the luncheonette counter in town. He never paid a bill in his life except with cash. When he got a check for a published story he gave it to Suzanne to deposit in the bank. An accountant made out their income taxes after Suzanne did all the paperwork for it. "I was always good at math so one year early in our marriage I did all the figures for our taxes and we wound up paying a steep fine for my errors and flagged for life." He constantly lost his keys to the house, so never carried them anymore. If the house was locked and nobody was home, he got the keys from under the front doormat. "Not the smartest place to leave them, but if the hiding place was any more secretive than that, I'd forget where they were." He used to know how to operate a TV set until the old one broke down and Suzanne bought a new one that needed a remote. "Don't ask me why," he once said, "but I know how to put a record on a turntable but not a CD into a cassette player, or where I can get it to work."

He still typed with only two fingers and his left thumb for the space bar. He liked to smell flowers but for years hasn't had the heart to pick them, he said, even in the unmowed small field behind his house. "I don't want to sound sensitive about this, since anyone who knows me will tell you that's one thing I'm not, but years ago I once picked this beautiful tall blue flower to surprise Suzanne with and thought I heard the entire field weep. No, that's gotta be bullcrap. It was no doubt the wind suddenly picking up and blowing through all those wildflowers and tall grass and weeds, and I should've just thought that." He also had a library card, he said. "How could I have forgotten that one other form of nonidentification I have. I've lost it I can't tell you how many times, and they always replace it free and without comment or fuss. I always take the card with me when I go out. I never know when I take a walk, if I'll end up there—it's about a mile away. If I'm walking Farrah and want to go in, I tie her up outside. I use their copier a lot for my new stories or old ones I got someone to retype because they were starting to look too shabby for even me to send out, but every time I do it I have to ask someone there to show me how to use the machine again. I also make a point of getting to the library every Thursday around noon when the new books have been catalogued and set out, so I can be the first to see what new fiction had come in. And sometimes I just like to sit in one of their fat padded chairs, with a newspaper or hanky over my face and surrounded by tons of sleepy books, and take a quiet nap."

Twelve years after Irv met Leonard, Suzanne threw him out of the house when she found out he was having an affair with a woman in town. Irv was married now and living and teaching college in Baltimore. Leonard met the woman while they were walking their dogs—she had three so small that she sometimes carried them in one arm at the same time. "At first," Leonard told him, "we bumped into each other accidentally about twice a week on the street. Our dog-walking schedules were almost identical, so it was just a question of which direction we started out when we left our houses. If I got to the end of my front walk and went left and she got to the end of her driveway and went right and we were walking at around the same pace, we'd meet up about halfway between our houses, which were eight blocks from each other. When we first started to meet we talked about our dogs and the neighborhood and why we chose years before to live on this side of the river instead of the more fashionable other, and what we did. I got lucky for a change, since she said she loved writers—any kind of serious artist. So you can say I started with a big advantage, especially when she learned I was something she'd never bumped into before, a published writer. After a couple of months of these accidental meetings, which I think on both our parts became less accidental as time went on—I mean, where was she before I'd started seeing her on her walks?—she suggested we have coffee in town at a new fancy coffee shop I'd never wanted to go to before... or I suggested it.

Makes no difference. What does is that we went there a few times a month, sort of made it our place, and then she invited me to her home for coffee—she's divorced with ten-year-old twins. We started having coffee there more than in town, and one thing led to the other. She read some of my stories, showed me some of her poems, a subject I knew nothing about. But I said—because if I didn't know anything about it but didn't want to say I didn't, what else could I tell her but this?—that I didn't know much about poetry and the little I've read I haven't much understood or liked, but I know for some don't-ask-me-why reason I like hers and maybe even a lot. She said I was too literary and bright not to know a great deal about poetry but that she liked it that I lied, though she won't tell me why. As for my liking her poetry, she said, she'd only be sounding like self-ridiculing me in arguing against it, so she'll keep her lips tight. Anyway, she'd feed me at her home these delicacies she picked up at a new gourmet deli and bakery in town. I had my first afternoon glass of chablis in my entire life. Also my first and last Jacuzzi bath—it's overrated as stimulation and if you want to wash yourself you can't really work up a lather in it. Then Suzanne got wind of my doings and ordered me to leave because the whole thing was too disgusting and humiliating for her. And it was, besides being beyond-belief stupid of me, busting up my not-so-hot marriage to shack up with this much younger and smarter rich doll, and I began living with her in what to me was an estate and helping her twins with their math homework." He lived with the woman for about a year. "What do you do if you bump into Suzanne?" Irv asked, and he said "If I see her in town or on a nearby street when I'm walking Farrah, I try to get out of her line of sight fast. She's caught me a couple of times before I could sneak away and ran up to me screaming and pointed her sharpened fingernails at my eyes and laid a curse on me that I shouldn't drop dead but instead should die a long and painful death, and the second time a similar curse because the first one obviously didn't work. No, I shouldn't joke about it, because I'm really sorry for what I did to her and made her feel. I'm serious now. I'm usually not, I know, but with this I am." The woman was so loaded, he said—she had her own family fortune and her stock-broker husband also chipped in a lot—that she paid for a two-week vacation for them on a Caribbean island. "I forget the name of it; they all sound the same, like a rum drink. She even paid to board Farrah in the best kennel in Rockland County while we were away." He hated the beach and sun there, so most of the day he hung around their luxurious hotel cottage, as it was called: "We even had our own small private swimming pool, shaped like a mermaid, where if we wanted we could swim nude because it was hidden from the hundred other back patios and private pools. I never used it, since I never learned to swim, but I did sit beside it with my feet in the water when the sun went away, and read and wrote. But unlike Suzanne, who called me weak-kneed for not braving the sun's rays more and maybe even going all out for the burns to toughen my skin, Brenda said I was smart to stay away from the sun because of what it could do to me." Going there really peed Suzanne off, he said, not only because he went with that woman but because he never took a vacation with Suzanne except once for two days at a cheap New Jersey beach motel in mid-winter so she could be near her favorite uncle who was dying, and the only reason he came along, she told him, was because it had the makings of a good short story, and it turned out it did, he said. Manfred, who was long out of graduate school by now and living home, refused to talk to him through all this, and whenever Leonard called him, he immediately hung up. "Though he said to me the first time I called 'What you did to Mom, screwing around with a rich pig a few streets from us, was the lousiest thing you could do short of balling the woman neighbor next door.' He forgot to say 'with the curtains open and a loudspeaker blaring your moans out the window into our house.' But again, serious: I told him he was right and I'm sorry but please don't reject me, but he has. Okay, good, he's on Suzanne's side all the way, which should be some comfort to her, and I'm being serious there too." Then Brenda sent him packing, he said—said she couldn't take living a day longer "'with one of the laziest and most selfish men alive.' I said to her 'When did you first discover that? I've been telling and showing you all along that that's what I am and that if you didn't take my word for it, you only had to speak to Suzanne.' Damn, why would she ever think I wasn't that way, since anybody could see that most of my fun came from, and same with my activity going to, just one thing: my cockamamie work, worthless as it might be." No place to live now and no money except his father's small monthly check and about five hundred dollars a year from story sales, he asked Suzanne if he could move back. "Legally, shot as the marriage was, we were still hitched and owned the house jointly. Though I promised if she let me stay there till I could somehow manage to rent my own place, I'd sign the whole joint over to her including, if she wanted, all the little magazines I was in the last twenty-five years that I keep under our bed." Manfred went to live with a friend when he heard Leonard was moving back, so Suzanne let him have Manfred's room to sleep and write in—"No more writing in the dining room," she told him, "and making that hideous racket with your typewriter and messing the table up." "Two separate bedrooms was okay with me," he told Irv, "since Suzanne and I had stopped sleeping together, if you'll excuse the expression, some years ago, except for a few times when she must have had a wet dream and woke up and forgot who she was in the same bed with. No sex was one of the reasons for my starting up with someone else. Another was that this woman wanted to start up with me, something that never happened before. By the way, what Brenda saw in me I honestly don't know. Sure, a writer, and she admired so-called real writers. But she's fifteen years younger than me and very pretty, with a nice figure, while I'm so much of a mess. I don't know how to dress. Half my clothes are discards from you. And for all I know, they smell, or even my body, though I try to take care of myself that way. I'm always in need of a haircut and most of the time my glasses are held together by surgical tape and miniature safety pins because I'm too lazy and embarrassed and short of dough to go to the eye guy again in town to get them fixed or replaced. I'm not fat but I'm totally unfit. Maybe my legs are good from all my walking and my fingers from the writing I do. I'm a shlub right down to my shoes needing heels and soles and I kept telling her she could do a lot better but not much worse, and she kept saying she's doing just fine. Till she got sick of me, as she should have long ago. She was bright too. Great lines all the time and she got most of my jokes. Read a lot. Could run circles around me in talking about literary theory, though so could probably any eighteen-year-old who took a freshman English course. Really, she knew more than me about any literature before the twentieth century other than for the first four hundred stories or so, or the ones translated, of Chekhov's and most of the other well-known nineteenth and twentieth century Russians. So: fine woman, great mother, wonderful companion, terrific cook, which unfortunately was wasted on me, and for all I know, a helluva poet. My one gripe was that she kept the house too neat and apologetically and uncontrollably used to sweep under my table and chair when I was writing and sometimes deep, for me, in thought."

Two months after he moved back Suzanne said if he was going to continue living there he had to pay half the house payments and his share of the other costs, especially food, utilities, and car insurance and repairs and gas if he wanted to be driven anyplace. "In other words," Leonard said, "I have to get a job and I haven't a clue where to look. Got any ideas?" and Irv said to try teaching. "You've no advanced degree or published book but you do have plenty of magazine publications and a couple of anthologies—enough, I'd think, if you didn't mind this at your age—and what's your choice except some other low-paying start-up job?—to become an adjunct somewhere and crawl your way up from there." Leonard got work at Hunter College and Fashion Institute of Technology teaching freshman English and expository writing. "I did what you told me to. Called all the colleges in Bronx and Manhattan. Asked the name of the English department chairman, dialed him or her directly and said I was a published fiction writer for thirty years and looking for a position teaching fiction writing. Two of them said they might have something open. I was interviewed—again, did what you advised: got a haircut, shoes shined, jacket cleaned, etcetera—and was offered both jobs. I thought I was lucky, even if I wouldn't be teaching what I know instinctively, till I saw what they were paying me. Both chairpersons assume I know all about pronouns and prepositional phrases and so forth, when I don't even know what expository writing is and can barely tell the difference between 'him' and 'he' when using the word 'between.' I just write what I write and if it's unintentionally sloppy and ungrammatical, I always thought that's what the editor's for. So now that you helped me get these jobs you got to show me how to teach this stuff and what self-help books to go to so I can learn as much as I can about writing good English and the rules of it." "How many classes you got this semester?" Leonard asked after about a month of teaching, and Irv said "'Courses' do you mean? Always two, plus a couple of independent students and this journalism internship program I run, not to mention all my advisees," and he said "Just two? I've got five, a heavy load for someone half my age. I'm already so tired from preparing and conducting classes and boning up on my freshman English and reading textbooks for the courses and a zillion student papers to read and writing corrections and critiques and hours of office conferences every week that I sleep on the bus going home and also on the subway, where I was so out of it once that I got my pants slashed and pocket picked without knowing it. And because of all that work and traveling I can't get a stitch of my own writing in, which is killing me."

Halfway through Leonard's third year of teaching he called and said "I got a promotion, or by my skimpy expectations it is. I'm just at Hunter now, so no schlepping back and forth between schools. Only four courses a week, with a tiny raise for each one, so I'm making around the same I was last term with one less course. But the real good news is I've been given an introductory fiction-writing course. It was between me and an English prof who once published a story twenty years ago in a good little magazine. But when he heard he'd have to be in school at nine A.M. to teach it, he told the chairman to give it to me." Two months into the new term he called Irv and said "I know the last thing you need to see is more manuscripts, but I wonder if you'd do me a big favor. I've this student in my writing class, an unbelievable writer, and I'm hoping you'll tell me what you think of her stuff. I've given her a few of your works to read and though she didn't like everything, she admires some a lot and that you get so much published. My opinion of her fiction's so high that I'm wondering if I'm also being a little influenced in that she's such a sweet person, with the most doll-like face you ever saw on this skinny twenty-six-year-old body that looks fourteen, and also that she's lived one of the crappiest lives I've ever heard of." Irv read three of her stories and said to him on the phone "First off, she's nothing personal to you, so that if I did say anything less than the most enthusiastic praise about her work—" and Leonard said "Me? Be offended? From you, never. Say what you want. She's my student, that's all." "Okay, then. She's good, but no better than half my graduate students. So I'd say—" and he said "She's an undergraduate, been writing for just two years. This is a starter course I teach," and Irv said "Right, I forgot. Then I'd say she's damn good for an undergrad and if she were one of mine—and I teach a wide range of courses for them over the year, from rudimentary to the most advanced—she'd rank with the very best. But like your favorite writer Chekhov said when—" and Leonard said "Babel's now my favorite, Chekhov next. But go on." "It was to a rich young woman who gave him her first two short stories to read and said something like 'Please, Anton Povlovich, tell me if there's anything there'... he said 'These are good and show some talent. So now—'" and Leonard said "No, I think in this case that's not what Chekhov would say. She's written way more than two stories. Close to thirty. So you wouldn't have to read too many pages, I only gave you the shortest ones. I've read most of them and they're all as good if not better than what you saw. And one very long one, which I especially didn't want to saddle you with— seventy-some pages; it should be the novella in her first book of a novella and stories—was so good that it kept me awake in the hour-long bus ride home after teaching when every part of me but that little nugget in my brain that loves good fiction was dying to sleep. It's true her stuff's a bit raw technically. Though her excuse, unlike mine, could be that she's only recently started college after a long layoff from getting educated, though she's a quick learner. She's six to seven years older than most everybody in class. And a rough life, as I think I told you. Poor and unhappy childhood from day one. But real bad, with every kind of abuse. I wouldn't be surprised if someone in her lowlife family didn't do something sinister to her in her incubator. She was born five pounds below average, by the way; weighed something like a hundred goose feathers. But beatings, locked in closets for entire days. No food for a day, for instance, because of petty arguments with her parents... I mean, they were crazy, as was her older brother, who ended up shooting himself after he tried to screw her. Plus a husband who repeatedly beat her head against walls and countertops, and she has a half dozen scars to prove it. But it gets worse: lost her only baby, which was three weeks due, when a mugger kicked her in the stomach. Then maybe a month later she almost died of cancer, but she's now considered cured. So she got into Hunter—they waived the high school degree requirement because of her life experiences, as they call it—while also holding down a full-time waitress job and living in a stinking hovel. If anyone deserves a break and also some money, she does, so I'm going to peddle her work to magazines and book editors. I know of a few people who, though no longer interested in me because I'm so out of it with my old-fashioned stories and prose and sensibility, might be into her because of her age and what she's gone through and writes about and, let's face it, she's a gal and women are the biggest readers and book buyers and run most of the libraries. And because I haven't had anything new of my own to send around in more than two years, I can concentrate on her work. She's publishable, no matter what you think—" and Irv said "That could be; I didn't say she wasn't, and of course I've read only a little of hers. Anyway, no reason why you shouldn't try, and I really hope you place something." "I think there's a good chance. Her stuff's got guts, almost like nobody else's I'm reading. To me it's like she slits herself open every time she writes and those guts just spill out, but in a certain order. That's what a writer should do, and both of us did, at her age and into your thirties, when I think one's best work is written because of a whole bunch of factors: experience, your technique's at its best, you still got plenty of energy to write while doing other things and haven't exhausted all your stories, and it's a sort of do-or-die time to make your big artistic break or just fold or coast." "I don't know," Irv said. "I still think I'm reaching my peak, or already reached one or two of them—for me, at least—and am going on to more. One's artistic life can be a mountain range instead of a monadnock, if you want to carry this analogy to—and I'm afraid I can't on the spot come up with a good substitute—absurd heights. Jesus, I don't think I ever said anything like that about myself, except to myself—you'll have to excuse me. Anyway, what I suppose I'm saying without all that mountainous crap is that I'm not done yet, I think. And when you finally get the time to write—reduction of your course load, for instance, but earning the same if not more money, or just not being so damn conscientious with your students—give them fewer assignments to write, that's what I do—neither are you," and Leonard said "Let's hope so; I'm a mess without it. But listen, getting back to this girl student of mine, could you send me your Hit List of places to send to—the one you make up for your grad students every year? Once more I lost the copy you sent me, and I've only a few names and addresses of magazines written down here and there, which I know I'll never find."

About a year later on the phone: "Remember that sweet young writing student I once spoke to you of, Tessie?" and Irv said "Yeah, you were sending her work around. I didn't know her name—but is that the one?" "Never could get anything of hers published, though I'm still trying. I'm living with her now," and Irv said "Oh boy, how'd that happen?" and Leonard said "I don't really know. Might have started early on when she seemed to have a crush on me. But I thought that's bonkers for me to think, even if I started having a little crush on her then too, but the stupid kind, of a geezer for a young girl. After all, Brenda—you remember her; that very nice woman who took me to the Caribbean and where I somehow avoided burning my back—was fifteen years younger than me and I thought then that was too much, but Tessie's almost twice that. The mutual silent crushes went on for a while, nothing else between us, when suddenly I'm sleeping with her after school at her apartment about every other week. Never told you because I didn't feel right about it and thought it'd end soon and that'd be it. But then it got to be once a week I'm riding the subway up with her to her place, and Suzanne, who I feel doubly worse about now, after Brenda and my having settled back in, is getting wind of it. More than wind. An anonymous caller—a guy's disguised voice—left a message about it on our answering machine twice. The first time I caught it—I actually learned how to play the messages back. Thought I had to in case one of my students called. I never learned how to erase, though, so I just tore the tape out of the machine and told her my student had spoken too fast and I was trying to rewind it by hand and fouled it up. But she got to the machine before me for this guy's next call. I felt I was bound to be found out after the first one, but fooled myself I wouldn't." "Who is this guy, someone who has the hots for Tessie or something?" and he said "I don't know but I assume he's read some of my work or sat in on one or more of my classes, by what he had to say about me. And he said the same thing in both calls, as if he had it written down, though saying beforehand the second time 'For Mrs. Fisk, in case you didn't receive my first message, which it doesn't seem you did, judging by the continued idiot postcoital grins,' or however you pronounce that word, 'of the parties involved, this is what I said on your answering machine last week: "Your illiterate husband's been taking unfair advantage of his authority, powers and age difference in a teacher-student relationship by shtupping what's comparable to a kid."' Suzanne played it for me, I denied, but she didn't believe me and threatened to scream her lungs apart and rip up every copy of every unpublished story of mine in the house till I told her the dirty truth. So I told her, since there's nothing I can stand less than her high-pitched hysterical shrieks; as for my stories, I had copies of all of them somewhere at work. I still don't know how anyone could have learned about me and Tessie unless she blabbed it around, which she said she didn't, or her priest did, since at Hunter we were the model of good behavior, and her apartment was miles from school and nobody knew me there. I told Suzanne I only shtupped her twice and both times, 'if you want me to be perfectly honest,' I said, 'I couldn't even get into the act because I knew what I was doing was so wrong, and the girl means nothing to me and it was just an older fool's last dumb futile attempt at a sloppy fling before he settled down with his wife for life, if she'll let him.' I'm a writer, so the one thing I'm good at is being a liar, though it was the truth I was saying about not seeing Tessie again and wanting to stay with Suzanne. She said 'Okay, but this is the last time I'm taking your crap, because once more and you're out of here forever,' and I told her 'I mean it, I swear.' For you see, by this time I'd long moved back to the main bedroom with Suzanne, though because of this new thing she exiled me from it for another month. I missed that room, lying on the only comfortable bed in the house and sticking my hand underneath it anytime I wanted to and pulling out one of the hundred or so magazines with my story in it. I even put together a story collection from the first twenty stories I blindly pulled out from under the bed and in the order I pulled them, called it *Chance*, but it didn't do me any better that my other collections did with a publisher." "And Manfred?" Irv said. "How's he doing?" and he said "Moved back when Suzanne and I resumed sleeping together and he could have his old room. Then out again during my exile month and back when Suzanne let me in her room again. Now he's gone from the area for good, he says, unless I leave it permanently, so he doesn't have to run into me by mistake. And also, which I really regret, that he'll never speak to me again no matter what I do to make things right with the family, because I'm such a rotten boob and have disgraced his mom and soiled their house and everything I touched in it," and Irv said "I'm sorry. And you never said, and don't if you don't want to, but how'd you finally end up with Tessie—no other place to go?" and he said "No, and it's quite a story, but too much like a bad romance movie so nothing writable. She moved to our town without telling me three months after we split up. You know, I'd see her at Hunter during this time and we'd smile or say hello but never stop for more than three seconds to talk. Then one day I'm walking the same route I always do to the post office in town—I guess she was watching and timing my movements, and Farrah's dead, by the way, so I now go alone—and there she is, standing on the sidewalk in front of this private house she took an apartment in not ten blocks from where I lived and on the same street. She's holding out a single long-stemmed flower for me, even though she knows flowers are about the last thing in my life. She put it under my

nose—this, before even saying 'hi'—and said 'Smell,' and I
held my breath and quote unquote smelled and she said
'So what do you think?' and I said 'As a gesture for everybody
in the neighborhood to see, it stinks.' She starts crying, so I
take the flower and say—but what's the difference what I say.
She's there, moved in, rent, she says, is half what her Bronx rat
trap was and she has twice the living space and a new kitchen
and a toilet that flushes without shit spilling out of it every
third time, and she just wants to be near me, if only with the
same zip code if that's all it can be. I tell her, after giving her
back the smelly flower, that she's crazy and should move to
another town. Actually, I said she made the wrong move,
because I can't have anything to do with her, including not
talking to her on the street. I want to save what's left of my
marriage and try to get my son back too, I tell her, and she says
that's all right with her then, since she likes it much better out
here than the city, even if she can't live with me or even see
me once a month. The sky, the trees and air. And the street's
quiet and the landlady and neighbors are wonderful, treating
her like a loving daughter. She always wanted to live in the
country, she says. And the bus to the city isn't expensive and
she can read all the way, as there's always a seat. She even,
with a clipboard and pen, gets some writing in during the rides.
Anyway, before you know it and for no discernible reason I can
see, since it wasn't as if I wasn't getting along with Suzanne or
that I was crazy in love with Tessie or even still infatuated with

her or got the hots every time I saw her, I'm in and out of her place almost every other day and Suzanne finds out and I'm cooked. I didn't even try to lie that I was there only to discuss her fiction in a mentor-protégé relationship and to help the poor kid out as her unofficial faculty adviser. Divorce, which I won't fight, since she's got the goods on me—witnesses. That surrogate mother of a landlady who took photographs for her from her front window of me coming and going and once even waving hello to her, not knowing her own upheld hand concealed a miniature camera. Suzanne also got a couple of her new gym pals to hang out in a car in front of Tessie's building and write down when I went in and how long I stayed, and the two other tenants there signed affidavits I wasn't visiting them. That left what? That I was always going to the basement to check the pressure gauge of the furnace? But because Suzanne was intent...*intent*; how do you like that word, and you also didn't say anything about 'affidavit' and 'discernible.' Teaching's made me so conscious of language and spoken words and, because I don't want to sound dumb in front of all those mostly unintelligible kids, a little more articulate, that it's almost sickening. Anyway, she was intent on destroying me. And since I'd already signed over our house and joint money accounts to her to let me back after that Brenda thing, I had to move in with Tessie for want of anyplace else to live. She's learned how to drive and bought a used car to get me around. What's really nice and a big change from what I'm used to, is she'll do anything for me, though there's nothing I want from her other than a place to sleep and a table to work on and a ride to the dentist or the bus stop or post office on a real rainy day." "How's your department taking it, you mixed up with an undergraduate?" and he said "Not bad. Suzanne called my chairman and told him about Tessie and no doubt made it seem as if I had forced sex, living arrangements and buying a car on her in exchange for an A grade and great recommendations. He called me in and said because Tessie's over twenty-five he didn't see how he could boot me out for moral reasons. Besides, he said, I'm doing the work of three teachers for the price of one and without complaint have taken on any extra unpaid-for work asked of me. 'Maybe all that makes you a tad stupid,' he said, 'but also irreplaceable to me for the time being.' He even talked of a permanent appointment in two to three years and putting me up for tenure in five or six, but probably only, he said, if she dropped out of school or I married her before she graduated."

About a year later Leonard called and said "Listen, I know you're not going to get offended by this or that I didn't even tell you, last time we met, that it was going to happen, but Tessie and I got married last week and didn't invite you to the wedding. She didn't want anyone at the ceremony but her immediate family and best friend, and them only because they wouldn't have understood not being invited, and also my dad and Manfred. My dad was too frail to leave the city and

Manfred didn't answer my invitation by phone or mail, so I suppose he still hates my guts." A few months after that Leonard said on the phone "You couldn't have called at a worse time. I only picked up the phone because I thought it was the ambulance service. They're coming to get us in fifteen minutes. Tessie's water broke, she's deep into what they call the right contractions, and she's dilated, she thinks, up around the big ten, so we're on our way to the hospital. This time no false alarms, as we've been there twice for this already and both times they said 'Too early, go home.' I wish I knew somebody close nearby to drive us, for these ambulance rides are setting us back plenty. I'm too old for this—too old to be a father again, I told her over and over. But once she talked her way past the fifth month, what could I do? She wants two, no less, but one at a time, and I told her one's more than I bargained for but I'll take it for her sake, and two she gets over my dead body. —I know, I know," he said away from the phone. "I'll hang up just in case they do call," and into the phone "You heard; gotta go. Wish us luck," and Irv said "I never knew about it; when did she get pregnant?" but Leonard had already hung up and Irv was glad he hadn't heard him ask such a dumb question.

They had a girl, and three years later, a boy. "I fought her having the second one tooth and nail; I almost thought we were going to split up over it. 'If I abort it, this could be my last chance to get pregnant,' she said. 'From now on I know you'll make sure I'll be more careful, even to dumping your seed on my stomach every time we do it, so I'm having the baby.' I told her just because I'm still able to get it up once a year doesn't mean I'm not too old to be a father again. Fathers have to hoist their kids to their shoulders, swing them around by their arms in some merry-go-round game, roll on the grass and get them down from trees and so on. All the things I never did with Manfred, but she wouldn't listen. If she doesn't inherit a fortune from her impoverished father and my own dad doesn't have a stash of stocks socked away he doesn't even know himself he has, I'll be teaching till I'm eighty to send my kids through college." "Speaking of Manfred," and he said "No, I thought I told you. With each new kid he hates me even more. But he got even with me for inviting him to my wedding four years ago by getting married a few months back and not inviting me to his. All our old friends went, the ones who won't talk to me anymore out of loyalty to Suzanne and no doubt also because they're afraid of her rage if they so much as say baa to me. Even my dad, who thinks I'm a first-class putz for refathering at my age, went to the wedding, but only because it was in the city just a few blocks from him and someone could cab him over. He told me all about it and what a nice gorgeous doll Manfred's bride is and what knockout grandkids I'll have who I'll never see. Suzanne sent me the wedding invite two weeks after the ceremony took place and wrote across it in thick red ink like blood 'See what you missed by being such a filthy despicable pig?'" Leonard got a three-year appointment at Hunter ("For all the work I do, that means I'm making peanuts instead of the beans I made in my year-to-year contracts, but I feel lucky to get what I got") and was put up for tenure a few years after that ("Okay, I started late and with only a simple B.A., so you're looking at America's oldest new assistant prof"). Tessie got pregnant a third time but miscarried. "I swear I had nothing to do with her losing it. My guess is the little guy picked up the message somehow what it'd be like living with me when I absolutely didn't want it, so shrank back and withdrew. From now on, if I don't use my own protection, I *will* be dumping everything on her stomach as she once said I would. If a sperm can make it from there to her uterus or wherever his lovemaking with the egg takes place, I'll accept the conception as something short of a miracle or at least out of my control, and learn to live with it." He and Tessie bought a house in town. "A small cheap one that needs lots of fixing up which we'll never do. But so cheap that even we could afford it and so small that all the furniture but the beds and my typing table will have to be photographed and the pictures blown up to life-size and tacked to the walls. Though it is just a few streets from the post office and the one store in town you can buy writing supplies. And it has a good view from the upstairs bathroom of the endless construction and the tieups from it on the Tappan Zee Bridge. At night the bridge is actually beautiful I can say— me, who thinks nothing truly is but a brand-new hickory baseball bat—all those slow-moving lights. We also have seagulls crapping on our roof and walks, which doesn't bother me since it shows how close we are to the Hudson and its breezes, and it's probably in some country's culture a sign of upcoming fortune and good luck."

Now what? Leonard's in a health care center in the Bronx near Co-Op City. "A dementia clinic is what it really is," Tessie said on the phone, "but they don't like calling it that. Most of the patients there are either walking around in circles for hours or sitting alone and not saying anything or talking to themselves a mile a minute. He seems a little better off than most of them. You can understand all his words clear enough at least—it helps that unlike most of his fellow immates, he speaks in English—though like them much of it is gibberish. He's more the walking-around-the-halls type than sitting alone, which goes with his personal history, I suppose. Honestly, I wish I could get him a dog for his long jaunts. But then when you think of it, his forty years of solitary writing should have qualified him for just sitting alone and composing crazy thoughts in his head all day. But his body can't stay still, face often twitching, feet tapping, hands usually jittery or flying around, never sitting for more than two minutes. I don't know if all that's because of his condition or the pills to relieve the symptoms of it. But whatever medication starts working then seems to give him something worse that needs new and stronger correction. It's a hopeless cycle, never upwards, unless you're talking about heaven, as it seems to be for almost everyone there. He even threatened—Leonard, the most noncombative person I've ever known—one of the nurses with his fists the other day when she tried forcing a handful of sedatives down him. He's aware enough to know he doesn't want to be knocked out by drugs and he had to be held down by Mr. Burly and Mr. Brawny, I call them, two oversteroided giants, and sedated more than he usually is. Good thing I wasn't there or I would have jumped on those giants and no doubt been thrown across the room and possibly arrested or sedated myself. I've got to get him out of that madhouse and into a less understaffed and gentler home. This one believes in putting its more obstreperous patients— meaning the ones who don't react well to repeated sedation overdoses—into restraints. Right now I don't see what choice I have of preventing them from treating him this way other than having him discharged, since our savings are gone and his father's dead"—"I didn't know that. I never met him, but I'm very sorry"—"and his second wife of two years got everything and we're living off Social Security and the little there is from his city pension, and Medicaid. I'm saying he's too much to handle alone at home, what with the kids and his irrational behavior and intermittent incontinence—I don't want to go in to what he sometimes does with his feces—and no public agency pays a nickel for homecare. At least with this place, till I find a better one that will take him despite our skimpy finances and his potential for violence, I'm covered and the kids and I are safe."

But lots of phone calls before that one. For instance one around a year ago in which Irv first learned of Leonard's condition. He called after a couple of months of not hearing from him and nobody picking up their phone and no response to his letters, and one of the kids answered. He couldn't tell if it was a boy or girl and had always forgot their names—one was named after a Danish queen who was sympathetic to the Jews during World War II, the boy after a famous Brooklyn Dodger outfielder of the Forties—and said "Hi, it's one of your dad's good friends; you and your family been away?" and the kid said "No, just in school. You want to talk to him?" and he said "Sure, but I'd also like to talk to you for a moment. Which child are you?" and the kid yelled out "A man wants to speak to Daddy, what should I do?" and Tessie got on and Irv said "Hey, finally; I've been trying to reach you guys for a while. Everything all right?" and she said "Leonard's not well. He's been weak for a long time, but always getting weaker, and had to give up teaching a month into the term. He couldn't make it through the class hour without feeling he was about to collapse and also in class questioning himself where he was sometimes and who are these fresh young faces staring alarmingly at him? He's on paid sick leave the rest of the semester. The chairman wasn't happy giving it; Leonard does so much work for the department that he didn't want to give him any inducements to stay away. He did say Leonard has the job for as long as he wants no matter how long he's out, but that his benefits stop at the end of the academic year unless he's teaching a full load the next one. I don't know what we'll do for money if he doesn't go back. I don't earn much, and if I have to look after him all the time, nothing will be coming in. Doctors haven't a clue what's wrong with him. Mono? Chronic Fatigue Syndrome? Nothing seems to fit. He took a battery of tests, red blood cells were up, white ones down, then it was the reverse or they went back to normal. So it seems nothing major, only mystifying, though he looks like hell. You haven't seem him for a while, but he's been losing weight steadily, and he just feels like sleeping half the time. He's sleeping right now, in fact. In a chair I sat him in a few minutes ago, book I gave him opened and about to fall off his lap. Said he wanted to read, but reading, like his writing, if you can believe this, he's done practically none of for months. Now his glasses are about to slide down his nose and off it, so I should grab them and also the book, while I'm at it, so he doesn't wake up when it crashes to the floor. I should also get his glasses adjusted to fit his increasingly thinning face. I've done that, adjustments, with his belt holes and also smaller jockey shorts and shirts. Only his shoes and socks are still the same size." "I know you have to go," Irv said, "but I want to tell you it's true Leonard and I haven't seen each other much the last two years, and I'm sorry about that. Just, when I do get to New York it's usually only for a day or a day and night to take Loretta to her doctors and that special clinic she goes to there, and in the evenings it's our only chance to see her dad." "How is she?" Tessie said. "But I really better hang up or it'll be another hundred dollars for new lenses we can't afford—he's trifocal—and then there's the kids and a million other things. Call again soon, will you?— he loves gabbing with you. But around this time or even a bit later, when the kids and I are usually home and can put him on. He has this new thing about phone rings and won't answer them anymore, even when he's here alone or with the kids and it may be me calling asking about them or him," and he said "I've called at all sorts of times. Now, earlier, evenings, and nobody's picked up for two months," and she said "Then I don't know. You may have been dialing the wrong number all this time, or the phone company's been screwing up again, crossing our line with someone else's—it's happened and I could tell you about all the stupid conversations I've heard because of it. If it's just the unlikelihood that our times haven't coincided in two months, then I suppose we should get an answering machine, though he'd only agree to one when they become extinct and replaced by some new invention."

A call a while after that: "Thanks for calling," Tessie said. "You're about the last friend left who does. You won't believe it: Lyme disease, that's what they diagnosed his whole debili-tated condition as, but not a clue about it till a few weeks ago. It never showed up on any test and he never complained of a bite nor did either of us see a sign of one, and it's gone to his brain. We've seen in the last month every kind of specialist there is for it but so far they've all come up blank for a cure. A nursing home, they say he'll need eventually—a year, two, at the most, three. That's how far things have gone with him and will go, and also heavy medication they say for what will be the problems coming from his worsening mental degeneration. For sure I won't be able to take care of him in six months without professional help during a lot of his waking hours. I've already looked into it. There's no way we'll be able to afford that much homecare. I don't know what to do. If I take care of him till he has to go into a home, which means learning to do most of the things a nurse does, then I can't work at a job. And if I don't work, where will the money come from once we deplete our savings?" Irv said "How could all this have happened so fast?" and she said "It can and did, Leonard's your proof. His condition's almost the same as Alzheimer's, in what it does and the speed it comes on—but Alzheimer's of the worst kind, seeing how fast he's deteriorated. You wouldn't believe how much memory he's lost just the last month. I mean, he knows me, the kids, he'll know you when I put you on, though I can't predict how much sense he'll make to you or for how long. He does things all the time now like turn the stove on to boil water for hot chocolate for the kids, something he always got a kick out of doing because it was so easy to do and gave the kids so much pleasure, especially with the baby marshmallows he threw in. But lately he forgets either the flame's on or to put water in the kettle or the kettle on the flame, so one thing or another burns or could if it's not caught. I've told him he can't use the stove alone anymore, or not until his memory gets better; the only other thing he used it for was to light an occasional cigarette. But I also won't let him smoke anymore except maybe outside where he can light it with a match, not only because of his stove problem but because he was beginning to forget he already had a cigarette or two lit. But he forgets he's not allowed to make hot chocolate anymore, or just gets so damn obstinate, and goes ahead. 'No stove,' I say, taking the kettle away, 'no stove for anything unless I'm here supervising it. You'll burn the house down. We'll all be dead or seared for life because of some stupid hot chocolate, nice as it is that you want to make it for them,' and of course he gets angry over this. All right, I could be a lot more tactful, but when our lives are at stake? Once I actually had to physically stop him from turning on the stove and oven both, because suddenly he was cold on a fairly hot day, and got a black eye out of it. But he did it by accident; my face got in the way of his fist." "Jesus," Irv said, "this just doesn't sound like him, not that I don't believe you," and she said "Wait, it gets worse. He goes into a fit every time I ask him if he's soiled his pants or when I tell him to take his smelly pants off so I can wash them. He does this—defecate unexpectedly—about once a week now. It used to be once a month, and a half year ago, never, and it's also so bad sometimes that I have to ammoniate whatever he's sitting on. Another sore point with him is the shower I insist he take right after it. He'll say why does he have to? He had a shower—*this* he remembers—that morning, which I always make him take, since he tends to leak overnight, and I say 'All right, here's why. That shower was before you crapped in your pants, so come on, get in.' But I now sit him on a shower chair because he's become so unstable on his feet sometimes that if he stands too long he'll fall. That's all I need: Leonard with crap on his backside *and* broken bones. I'll be honest; the future with him scares the daylights out of me. How do *you* handle it?" "Well," Irv said, "so far as the broken bones go, we've had those—nose, ribs, both her hands but at different times, and I can't recall how often she's cracked her skull. So we go to Emergency, or for the smaller skull cracks, I take care of it at home. But there's less chance of those kinds of accidents now since we got a new wheelchair she's strapped into with a seatbelt. We also had our bathroom redone over the summer where I can now roll her into the shower on a shower chair rather than lift her off the wheelchair and sit her in a chair in our old shower stall. I still have to lift her from wheelchair to bed to rolling shower chair, or transfer her as it's technically called, and then back into the wheelchair or bed once she's showered. But it's much safer and easier if you don't have to literally carry her from one chair to the other inside a cramped bathroom with sharp fixtures and metal hardware sticking out all over the place, plus the tile floor if she falls. True, there've been minor accidents—usually cuts on her legs—when I transfer her from wheelchair or rolling shower chair to toilet, but nothing like before." "I wish we could afford doing that to our bathroom," she said, "because I'm sure the time's coming when we'll need it." "There's also the customized van we got a couple of years ago, I forgot to mention, which has a fold-out ramp. With the old one, when I lifted her into the front passenger seat she often bumped her head on the door frame or fell over before I got her buckled in and hit her face on the dashboard. The new one, she just sits in the middle of it in her wheelchair, which is held down by floor restraints so the chair doesn't move." "All that's good. One after the other, you're doing the smart thing. The special van, which I'm sure cost you plenty, we fortunately don't need. He gets in and out of the car with ease and sits fine in his seat, and I don't see why that should change. Most of the time when I drive him even a mile, and when moments before that he was frenetic, he just sleeps. And your laundry? I know that sounds peculiar, but I'm talking about the other work you have to do. Because between the sheets and his leaks and accidental defecations, I do three washes a day." "You're doing one more wash a day than I," he said, "but then we also both have two kids at home. Though the clothes my girls wear have to be a lot larger than the ones your kids do, so they take up more space in the washer. On the other hand, your kids must soil their clothes faster than mine because they're so young, and Leonard's much taller than Loretta, so that probably equals it out. But then again, I'm much taller than you and no doubt change my clothes less often—I wear the same pair of jeans for three to four days and a pair of socks for two—so your three washes to my two sounds right." "On something else," she said. "I don't suppose you have problems with the stove and possible fires and things with Loretta as I do with Leonard," and he said "Oh, we're pretty prone to cooking mishaps like letting food burn or boil over. But major accidents by her we probably avoid because we got a new gas stove. It cost, but is worth it, since the controls are reachable for her now as are the back burners, just as the controls and shower nozzle of the shower are. We thought of also getting for that shower a computer-operated, I think, control that regulates the water temperature so it never scalds, but it was way too expensive. As for the old stove, it was electric and the controls were in back. She had to poke at them with her reacher, so usually ended up having to ask me or one of the kids to make her a simple tea, which she found dispiriting. Anyway, it's obvious things aren't anywhere near as difficult for me as they are for you, in just about everything."

Another call: "You know," Irv said to her, "I forget you were a writer. Leonard used to say great things about your work when you were at Hunter, and how much you wrote too. Still going at it?" and she said "You kidding? First of all, living with a compulsive writer and hearing him click away on his

tinny typewriter all day did in a lot of it for me. And then there
was holding down a regular job while helping to raise two small
kids, because Leonard, when he had all his faculties, was a
great dad. Now that they're in school, it's his sickness that
occupies most of my time. If I did stop giving myself excuses
and sat down to write, I doubt it'd be about anything but his
condition and rapid worsening of it and my taking care of him,
since that's how much it dominates my mind, and who'd want
to read such depressing material as that? Though you write
about your wife's sickness a lot, Leonard used to tell me. Since
I had the kids I've sort of lost interest, while also not having
much time for it, in reading, so haven't kept up with your
work. Leonard read whatever published stuff of yours you sent
him—books, magazines. I'm serious when I say he used to go
to bookstores looking especially for magazines you didn't send
him but said you were in, and if he found one he'd read your
work standing up in the store. For you, maybe writing about
your wife is more interesting or liberating than it'd be for me
writing about him. You can also give it to her to read for feed-
back and permission for you to write about her that way.
I can't anymore so I'd feel guilty writing about him in his
condition without getting his say-so. Also a bit qualmish what
he'd do if he ever had a sustained lucid period—I'm speaking
of a few hours—where he'd read what I wrote about him and
understand it. I suppose I could tell him 'Listen, you wrote
about me for our entire marriage and before that about when

we were slyly seeing each other and you were still married. All of it showing to the world, or to your limited readership, my worst machinations and foulest habits and moods, so I think I'm justified in writing about you for the first time.' Though he'd probably say, if his lucidity held out that long, 'My illness is my material, so at least leave me that if I'm to get anything good out of it and what it's done to me.' And he could be right, no? Your wife writes poetry, or did, Leonard said, so how does she feel about you writing about her condition?" and he said "She's resented most of what I've written about her, even when she was healthy. She wishes I'd fictionalize her more. Simple changes: turning her into a man and where the narrator's a woman with two boys and a dog. She also probably figures—I don't give her any of my work to read while it's being written, and if it's published I don't push it on her or ask her to volunteer what she thinks—that it keeps me relatively content from day to day just having something to work on, as I know was the case with Leonard. So, in balance, considering all I do for her—stuff I never thought I could deal with, though I actually did some of the same things for my father for four years—it's almost worth it, she might think, even if what I write at times can I'm sure be a little embarrassing for her. Or a lot. But I could be wrong about what she thinks. I never ask and so far all I've gotten from her is that muted criticism given as advice to disguise the wife's identity and condition more. The truth is I feel ashamed about some of the grislier and more graphic things I've written about her, though that's not going to stop me from doing it, or hasn't yet. Would I stop if she pleaded with me to and said something like nothing makes her unhappier, other than her illness, than some of the things I've written about her? I don't know but I don't think so, though I might put that work aside for a while—the grislier material, I'm saying—till I was able to convince her to let me try to publish it and without changes other than what I'd normally make to improve it after a certain time's elapsed since it was written. Sounds awful, my attitude on this, doesn't it?" and she said "It's not one I'd embrace if my writing ever came to that. If Leonard said he didn't like what I wrote about him, I'd change it till he was satisfied or get rid of it. If he wasn't able to understand what I wrote no matter how many times I read it to him—and I would, to give him a chance to reject or accept it—I'd put it away till he was dead and then maybe wouldn't resurrect it till years later. But then I haven't, by any stretch of the imagination, been writing as long and hard as you, so haven't got your experience in things like this, nor is writing and publishing as important to me anymore. That's not making a judgment, by the way, and may even be an indication of a fear I have about what I write that a writer can't have if she wants to write and publish. No, I amend that. Morally, I just can't justify it, I'm sorry. If you think the piece is going to hurt the person, you've got to get that person's approval to publish it. If the person's dead, then as a sign of respect—we're not talking about someone you dislike, you know—you have to change it around to where it doesn't look anything like her." "Okay," he said, "but you got to know that all that you said isn't going to stop me either. One could say I've been incorrigible like that for the last forty years. Or thirty, because the first ten I did what I could to respect the feelings of the people I was writing about, if I knew them, and also to get published. I'm not saying I'm proud of the last thirty that way, but I can't say it's been hard to live with. Of the first ten... well, I was still green as a writer, and regarding the publishing thing, thought I could make some dough from my writing then. Anyway, unless you have anything to add, is Leonard around and can I speak to him?"

Another call two weeks later: after she told him how Leonard was doing, he said "I was thinking, after our last talk when you said you wouldn't publish, if you couldn't get Leonard's permission, the more revealing things you wrote about his illness. But what about the people closest to you in the past? Would you publish something revealing about them without asking their permission, the ones who are still alive, and if you haven't received their permission, the ones who are dead?" and she said "If I understand your questions correctly, my answer is why would I want to? There has to be some tension, drama and story if you're going to write something, doesn't there? And ninety-eight percent of my life, before Leonard, was wonderful and comfortable and stress-free, but as material for fiction it was uneventful and mundane. I had a smooth birth, a happy childhood, an easy adolescence, a pleasant teenage period, and so on, till my mid-twenties when I met Leonard. Then my life became complicated, adventurous and a bit strange. And now this happened to me where it all went wrong and it became disturbing," and he said "What about your first husband—excuse me, but Leonard told me this—who mistreated you badly, he said. And your parents—" and she said "What?" and he said "There was something with them too. Abandonment when you were young—just one of them maybe—or your father dying early, or even something worse…it was a while ago when he told me. Locked in closets; being starved for a day or two sometimes? And something about a brother who was institutionalized, I think," and she said "I meant, what are you talking about? I told you: almost nothing but happiness when I was young. And no other marriage; Leonard's my first. And I've one sibling, a sister, who has never been anything but sweet as candy to me and sane and sensible as can be. She didn't want me marrying him, in fact. Said he was too old for me and I'll end up nursing him when he gets feeble and sick from age. I told her he'll outlive us all and be in stellar health till his clock runs out when he's a hundred. That he'll die peacefully in his sleep or when he momentarily forgets where he is and gets hit by a doubledecker bus in London while crossing the street and looking the opposite way. That's what I really thought then.

He told me he escaped every illness known to children, had never even had a cold. That the last medical exam he had was a routine one when he was fourteen, and he hasn't lost a day because of sickness in forty years. Was he kidding me? I know he never till now, since I met him, was sick or down with anything. If Leonard told you any of those things about me, then it's from a short story or cycle of them he wrote and which I've never seen, but with my real life radically changed," and he said "That could be but I don't recall reading a story of his with that material about you in it." "Maybe he couldn't get them published," she said. "And then, like about a hundred other stories of his written since we met—the ones repeatedly rejected—he put them away, saying he'll go over them another time and compile them into a few unpublishable collections, and now I don't even know where they are." "Under his bed, I bet," Irv said, "or is that where he threw the magazines he was in?" and she said "Not since I've known him for either, so first I'm hearing of it." "With Suzanne, then. Different bed. Maybe closer to the floor. But he definitely used to speak of it and squeezing his hand underneath to retrieve them, probably the magazines. But is he around, Leonard, and in good enough shape to talk to me?" and she said "He'd love to, though good luck in getting a conversation going with him," and yelled "Leonard, phone call; and kids, one of you, pick up for him."

Another call: "Thanks for the *Times'* article on Lyme disease," she said, "especially for the part about what it can do to the brain. Beautiful, huh? His doctors know all about the treatments described but said a while ago he's past being helped by any of them now or in the near future either, which I think means never. Only if there's a sudden breakthrough in drugs or surgery for acute Alzheimer's victims will there be any hope for him, but no one's expecting that too soon. So for now it's all downhill for him, till he can't stand anymore and has trouble swallowing and breathing on his own and keeping his food in, and forget memory, and then is finished. I'd in fact want him dead then, they tell me, and if he had any sense at the time, that's what he'd wish for most too. Sometimes I don't know why I don't break down when I speak of him like this, but it might be the same with you. Too busy doing our work for them, so we haven't time to fall apart," and Irv said "Oh, I have my moments, plenty, but never crying ones. Usually just hysterical fits where I kick or hit or throw something and curse and scream, mostly curse. 'Godalmighty, goddamn, f-ing shit, I can't stand any more of it,' because it's about when the chores seem unending. Or it's one disaster after the next and I'm tired or exhausted, and because I am, I start spilling and dropping things more than I normally do. After the fit, I only feel some relief if nobody's heard me, which isn't easy because I've been bitching about all the work I have to do for her while she's been in the same room or I'm shouting this stuff from the next one, or anyway, so she can hear me. Then I feel even worse than before, and if she cries or gets angry I either get sad for her or go into another fit because I can't face her anger and sadness. 'What're you crying for?' I'll say. 'I'm the one who oughta be crying, but who's got the time to?' which goes back to your original point. So now you know what a schmuck I can be. I'm sure it's nothing like that with you," and she said "I'm not lying when I say it isn't. Listen, Leonard can't come to the phone now. We should get a portable phone, but if we did he'd drop it down the toilet. He's on the potty—a fruitless pursuit too, it's becoming, but which takes an hour or two to find out. Future mess? Oh God. How about if you call back tonight, or we'll call you? Though he likes it much better when people are calling him. Makes him still feel part of things, what can I say? So I'll tell him you'll call, though you don't have to. But just telling him will make him happy, even if a minute later he won't remember I mentioned you. Which gives me an idea. Maybe I should tell him that a lot and say other people he knows also called him, just to get that fleeting rise out of him," and he said "I don't know. I'd hate to fool anybody, even if it's for the good and to someone who most likely won't understand he was fooled. I'll call later," but he didn't feel like it that night—actually, had very little time to because he was so busy with his wife and fixing dinner and doing a second wash and reading his students' manuscripts and driving his younger daughter to the library and picking her up, and then, though he thought of it a few times, didn't call for around two weeks.

"I'm sorry I didn't call back when I said I would," he said

to Tessie. "Got tied down right after I spoke to you and then I
don't know what the next few days, but almost constantly busy.
You know what it's like, but I still should have tried harder
to make the time," and she said "Don't worry about it, and you
couldn't have called at a more propitious time. We literally, a
minute ago, stopped talking about a letter of yours from last
month that I read to him for I'd say the fourth time. It
provoked some recognition of events that it didn't the other
times I read it. Usually, he just smiles and quietly enjoys your
letters. He said, for instance, regarding your reminiscence of a
reading you two gave at a SoHo bookstore twenty-five years
ago and where only one person showed up, and that person,
you both agreed, only there for the free eats, 'I remember that.
We alternated. He read, I read, he read, and I finished. Two
short-shorts each.' Was that really how it went, and also the
store manager in his introduction, Leonard said, getting your
names crossed?" "The names' mix-up I don't remember, but
he could be right. As for the other, I know it was Leonard's
idea we alternate, or maybe that was at our only other joint
reading, which a friend of his arranged in that small county
college near your town and where six people came this time,
including the friend and his wife and teenage son and the
woman I was seeing, the one who introduced me to Leonard."
"But the order he gave, when you did alternate, you're not
certain of? It'd be interesting to see how close he got to what
happened, particularly something so distinctive," and he said

"No, but it seems he got close enough. Anything else he comment on from my letter?" "When I asked if he remembered any of the other things you mentioned doing with him around the same time, because I wanted him to talk about them, he pointed to his head and said slyly 'What do you think? It's all here.' Also, he liked the account of your recent string of misfortunes. Your van again, that heavy barbell dropping on your big toe. 'Oh boy,' he said, 'that must have hurt.' The can of colossal-sized olives falling out of the cupboard on your head. And all on the same day plus, for a top-off, your toilet stopping up and that line you used which he got a kick out of: 'Forget the wheel. The plunger, the world's greatest invention.' Then he suddenly got serious, seemed about to cry, and said 'We shouldn't be laughing. It's no easy life, a writer's, as much if not more so when he's not writing.' That's as deep a remark as he's made the last few months, even if it didn't completely apply to what you were saying in your letter. But I'll take anything he said like that as a sign his brain's doing something other than deteriorating and that perhaps it's even making a turn for the good. But you can tell me, if you like, that I'm being pathetically optimistic and impractical," and he said "Why? Since he only has symptoms of Alzheimer's and not the disease itself—and they really, from that *Times'* article a while back, don't know for sure what the Lyme disease might do to his system and brain—it could be a good sign, it definitely could." "Oh, you're just saying that to make me feel

better and also to show I haven't begun losing my marbles,"
and he said "No, I never do that, or hardly, but not when
I catch myself. Instead of buttering up people or making with
the feel-good talk, and if I think the truth or what I can make
of the matter, hurts, I don't say anything. Honestly, that's what
I do." "Okay. And I should get Leonard to the phone before
this propitious moment stops." She came back about five
minutes later and said "He says, and these are his exact words,
because he made me write them down and to say that this,
finally, is his delayed response to your letter, 'It's not you, it's
not me, and I know you, but as you can a-b-c, I'm not in the
mood. Write more. Tragedies can be funny.' I'm sorry. And you
know he wasn't being rude to you. It does seem that turn he
made I spoke about before has been turned back. Call again
soon." "What'd he say again?" but she'd already hung up.

His next call a few days later: "Thanks for calling," Tessie
said. "I thought the last one might have put you off, but I
should have known better. Leonard appreciates them too,
as I know he's told you when you do get to speak to him. He
always seems to feel less depressed after he gets off the phone
with someone he knows well. Not with my sister, though.
She's been nothing but super kind and patient with him, but
after the last time they spoke he said 'Your saint sister, the
prophet. She hates my guts and wants them cut up and fed to
kosher pigs and me to die and my body to be crucified and
then burned at the stake. Don't put me on with her anymore.'

I won't, if she disturbs him so much, but he's wrong. And 'prophet'? He must have overheard me on the phone, when I thought he was napping, saying she predicted I'd end up nursing him. But you and she are among the few people who continue to call and want to speak to him. It's good for him to talk to someone other than me and the kids. And they go to him less than they ever did, and even hide from him sometimes because of his occasional rages and strange looks, and even the sloppy way he eats, though his table manners were never great, and everything like that. His clothes; fewer showers. I have to order him at times to sit in one because he stinks, and he'll say 'Why? I don't smell anything.' I mean, your wife, though I never met her but from everything Leonard and you have said, is probably levelheaded as ever and I'm sure hasn't let herself go as he has," and Irv said "No, no, shower a day, still very fastidious table manners and with her clothes. Of course her dexterity and such have been affected, so she compensates: pays closer attention, does things slower." "But getting back to what I was saying, since I don't want to seem like Leonard, flitting from one unrelated subject to the next and never finishing a thought—have you noticed in your own situation that when a spouse gets sick over a long period and has what seems like a lifetime or near-to-one disease and in my case looks like hell, people stop calling and coming around? It's as if—and I'm not referring to dinner invitations. Those we never got or gave many of and even if we got one today we'd have to refuse for the obvious reasons. But it's as if we no longer exist except to the medical people he sees and a couple of friends like you. You'd think others we knew well or he did would want to visit or at least call him, and if they can't even do that, me, to see how he is. A few of his Hunter colleagues, for instance, or his chairman he worked like a dog for. And a secretary in his department he was really tight with and whose job he saved by speaking up when she was about to be axed, I swear. Or if this is what has to do it to make them call or drop by, to think of it as an unpleasant task but the right thing to do for old time's sake. And maybe, if it's possible anybody would think this, to visit for half an hour just to take a little of the pressure off me," and he said "Actually, not that we were the most socially active people, though Loretta would have liked us, meaning me, to be more, we're down to about one couple here and another in New York, my wife's best friend. I've often thought—the dinner invitations being turned down or not reciprocated after we had the same people over a couple of times, or being given one excuse after the other why they can't meet us at a restaurant as they used to—that it was because of Loretta's disability and general deterioration and something with her looks perhaps and her wheelchair and everything they imagine might go on in it, if you know what I mean. So what's so new about that? People—not all—feel uncomfortable, or maybe that's not the right word for it—are frightened and even repulsed at serious life-threatening illness in other people, or of someone confined to a wheelchair. Also, they're worried about the problems involved in continuing to see us. How do they get her up their house stairs in a chair? If it's five to six steps, I can do it; it's what I've been working out in a gym for the last three years. And then, where does she sit at the dinner table? Will she make a mess? Break a valuable wine glass or plate? Suppose she has to go to the bathroom? Let's face it: will she piss or shit while they're sitting next to her? Or choke on her food? She's done that twice in the last two years. So I now cut her meat into little pieces and had to learn the Heimlich method. But so far, the last time, at a wedding reception, no less, someone beat me to it, a registered nurse who was also a guest there. Pushed me aside. Threw me, actually—I obviously hadn't started to do it right—and popped the piece out of her mouth in a few seconds. Or drool, which she never does, or hasn't since a pump was implanted in her to regulate the anti-spacticity medicine she takes. Goes directly to the spinal cord now, bypasses her brain. I think that's it. I'm constantly asking her what the various procedures she's had done and medications she takes do for her, and she invariably says or I can see she's thinking it: 'Why, are you writing something else about my illness?' So I try to hold back on the questions, or ask them cagily—'You know, I still don't quite understand what the pump in front of your stomach was put in for and if it was really worth it'—since I usually *am* asking because I'm writing something about her. I want to get it down right. But a lot of these things I'm talking about—jerking, losing control of one sort or another, dozing off several times a day and often at the dinner table, no energy, sudden crying jags, once even a runny nose that wouldn't stop—are brought on by drugs she's taking to relieve something else or the way it's dosed. You must have had something like that with Leonard." "Oh, have I," she said. "A drug for depression made him psychotic. The antidote for it turned him into a zombie. Another reduced his white blood cell count so low that for a few hours I thought he might die. His doctor said after 'So, we found out that one didn't work,' and I practically screamed at him 'Didn't work!' I didn't tell him what I really felt because there are very few specialists we can go to for Leonard's illness. One doctor said of a drug he wanted to try out on him 'It's true,' when I asked of the possible side effects. He can have a fatal stroke, he said, or just one where he loses his memory and thinking processes entirely— he used a more scientific term—but that's relatively rare, maybe five percent. No, thank you. He's been delirious, hallucinated, lost his ability to speak, been constipated for two weeks where even the hospital had difficulty unimpacting him. He's also had dizzy spells, kept falling, and once turned into such a savage satyr that there was no slaking him for days except with a combination muscle relaxant/sleeping pill, all because of different medicines he was given to counter, as you said, another disorder," and he said "One time Loretta went into shock from some drug," and she said "Same with

Leonard, almost a coma. I think I told you about it," and he said "No, I don't remember. With Loretta, I was in the hospital waiting area when it happened." "Same with me," she said, "same with me. Hopeless and helpless." "I wasn't even aware what was taking place, and they didn't come to inform me. Too busy reviving her, perhaps. Till they wheeled her past me on the gurney and I thought 'Oh good, it's over, we can go home now,' for she'd been in there for three hours, and I looked at her and she looked like a corpse. But a smiling one. She didn't, catch this, want to—she admitted this later—make them feel bad or as if they'd done anything incompetent. You see, she didn't want to give them an additional reason to give up on her as a subject for future clinical trials of different new drugs they were testing, or new use for an established one that hadn't been approved for this kind of treatment yet. I'd told her not to be a participant in it. But she was a prime candidate, they said. And if it had worked—it didn't, or five years later is still being tested—but with repeated doses of it over a year, it was supposed to have reconnected or rebuilt the nerve synapses or sheaths or something in her neurological system damaged or destroyed by her disease. Come as close to arresting it as anything yet conceived. She might even be able to walk with a cane or walker, they said. But she shouldn't get her hopes up just yet, since she might be given the dummy medication. And if she's given the real stuff there's always the chance it won't have that great effect on her, but they're pretty hopeful it will. They've had astounding results on rodents and in record time, they said. I'd told her that being a subject in such a trial was fine for people at death's door from the disease—you know, everything to gain, etcetera—but that wasn't her. Wait'll the drug's been proven on these people and has worked all its kinks out and so on, and then take it. No, she wanted to have her chance before her condition got even worse, since the FDA might ask for more and longer tests and not give its okay to the drug for years. She, it turned out, was supposed to have been given the placebo in this double-blind testing...you know what that is?" and Tessie said yes and he said "Good, because it's so complicated, at least to my mind, that it'd be almost impossible for me to explain it. Anyway, she got the real stuff by mistake and something went awry with it, as they said. They were extremely sorry, told us we knew there were risks with any experiment like this—it certainly wasn't the quality of the drug that was at fault, they said, nor, except for the switcheroo, the handling. If she still wanted to, they said, she could continue as one of their guinea pigs in the test though of course they couldn't guarantee she wouldn't really get the placebo this time. Even the people conducting the tests don't know who gets which till after it's completed, but with her they found out what she'd taken the first time because of what it did to her. From then on they were going to give lower doses to all the subjects. That would mean there'd be little likelihood of anyone going into shock again, if that was what might be keeping her from continuing in the experiment. And of course they also said that something very positive came out of it—determining what dosage was too high for one subject and thus correcting it for all—so it wasn't a total loss and she'd play an important part in the paper they'd write about their findings. She was game to go again, but I told her 'Over my dead body.' That didn't persuade her, so I said 'Then I'm sorry, but possibly over yours. Don't be an idiot,' I told her. 'You could be prone to shock with any amount of this drug in you, and next time it might lead to cardiac arrest or something like it. Don't listen to the great scientists. For that's what they are,' I said, 'your highly regarded chief doctor and his cadre of associates and assistants: interested in scientific statistics as much as living humans and also more and larger grants to continue their research. This is a big important specialized project they're involved in and you're only another body to them. Or more than a body—I'll give them that— but if you go into shock again or die they'll know how to soft-pedal it to themselves and explain it away to the hospital they're doing it in and future grants committees. "You lose some," they'll say. "Even GPs have to face that fact. But we'll never again take on a fifty-plus-year-old white woman with blondish hair and blue-green eyes and average height and two young daughters and a mean cat and a husband who's virulently skeptical of the motives of our work and feelings for our subjects in the tests, despite that the chief doc and lead associate kiss the women patients' cheeks hello and good-bye every time they come to the clinic."'" "So she didn't participate in that trial again?" and he said "She had to cave in to me once in her life, for never have I been so fierce and adamant with her." "Probably a good thing too, though I think your reasons against her doing it went, shall we say, a tiny tad overboard? I doubt I'd be able to stop Leonard if he wanted to be in an experiment like that. Mainly, he's so pigheaded, even when he's not all there. But he's always had this thing, which is ingrained in his brain by now so able to overcome any form and level of dementia, of not listening to me when I'm making especially good sense. Though he's never expressed a desire to be a subject for anything, including those telephone marketing surveys we get almost every other week. He used to hang up on them in seconds, when he still felt like answering the phone. 'We only take personal calls here,' he'd say; bang! Or, 'Before you say another word, let me talk to you about Jesus.' He knew they only wanted to see what you like so they can rent your name to outfits that sell whatever garbage it is. You're right, though, about some of it. In research hospitals— oh, any of them, and we've been to a few—some doctors can be so self-serving, careless and rude. Prescribing drugs that send him banging his head against the wall. Talking to him as if to a nincompoop. Sometimes not even addressing or looking at him when they're discussing his illness and what treatment they've mapped out for it. Only talking to me, though he's two feet across the table from them and so close to me I'm holding his hand. He knows the score a lot of the time and can see what's going on, I'm almost sure of it, and it's got to hurt. 'So this is all I am?' he could be thinking. 'Someone who's simply referred to and all the important decisions about my life are left out of my hands?' I don't know, though, what goes on in his head most of the time. He might look like next to nothing is, but his thoughts could be fairly deep and complex. Just that he can't express them or even give a sign, other than a pained look at times, that they're there. He might even be afraid to express them, because he knows how clumsily they come out. I've asked him about it—'What's going on in your noodle right now, Leonard?' and he always says 'What're you talking about? Don't be dumb.' You probably don't have most of these problems with your wife," and he said "For a long time she slurred and lost track of her thoughts and what she was saying, but for the last year—I'm sure I've told you—with this new treatment and such, her speech and thinking have improved tremendously. Even her handwriting; everything but her legs. So I suppose I owe something to these doctors other than money. No, I do." "With Leonard, no improvements no matter what he takes. And a few of his doctors have been pleasant and not at all self-serving and mercenary. One wanted to discuss books with him. Especially by writers who had gone through medical school and whatever it was in Keats's and Rabelais's days, but Leonard seemed too far out of it then, so she didn't get very far with him. Another said he always wanted to write a novel. That he did well in college English and took a creative writing course because he was pursuing this girl who was in it and got an A, but that he never, first with his medical studies and now his duties, had the time. I'm glad Leonard didn't feel like or was unable to answer him, because his old line when laypeople told him that was 'Leave writing to writers. Do I take up the scalpel or try to fix my plumbing? Besides, it takes years of plugging away before you can get anything good written.' And another woman doctor phoned me after a recent clinic visit to see if we got home all right. Leonard had acted like a lunatic in her office. Kicked over a chair, went into an uncharacteristic spurt of cursing, wanted to throw a paperweight, which had photos of the doctor's kids in it, through a door window. Took the two of us and an aide to restrain him. He was frustrated; so what else is new? He hates being so sick and out of it and that moment must have been one of the ones I spoke of where he saw how bad off he was and how he was rapidly getting worse and where he was probably never going to get better. If you were in his shoes you might, or maybe you're just too innately good-natured, throw the paperweight too. I know I would," and he said "Me? Good-natured? Now this I know I told you. I have a lousy temper. I'd throw and have thrown it for much less. Loretta can get like that too, but mostly tears, can't talk about it, never throws anything. I often have to force myself on her—pushing her pushing arms away and get her in a hug and kiss her head to console her—and after a while she feels better." "Leonard, if I tried to hug him when he's in that state, I think would punch me. And no pushing his pushing arms away, since he's still too damn strong and might grab my hand and twist it off." "But the doctors and hospital staff," he said, "—what we were talking about before? Some have been very nice too, helpful, professional, all that. So I was exaggerating how awful and cynical they are, though not entirely. And the plunging white blood cells you also mentioned before? Same thing happened to her with another drug they gave. Did I tell you this, since I seem to be repeating myself a lot lately?" and she said "Sounds familiar. But our situations are so similar sometimes, so who knows. Go on." "It was an infusion, nurse-supervised, but this one an FDA-licensed drug, thoroughly tested and at worst was supposed to give a headache for two days. She was so sick and such an infection risk after it that I wasn't allowed to kiss her for a week," and she said "You did tell me, but the kissing part's new." "And I remember another reason why we're down to two couples as friends on the entire East Coast and maybe one more for a month when we get to Maine in July, and that's that there are their other guests to think about, right? That couple who had us to their daughter's wedding, and Loretta choked, found that out. Of course she takes all the blame on herself. Says things like 'They don't know what to expect from me anymore. They think I've lost all control because I'm a cripple and don't even like looking at me while they're eating.' That's why, when these dinner invitations were still trickling in, I made sure to sit next to her at the table. Not just to cut her food but so she'd have someone to talk to. We discussed this a few times. Why old close friends cut us off when they seemed to like our company before. Maybe not mine as much, but they had to hers. I'm not big on spouse-boostering, but for the sake of argument she's a great person to have at a dinner party: smart, educated, well-read, up on a zillion things, cultured, and when her speech isn't affected by her illness, very articulate. She's the real teacher in the family—I know I already told you that, almost in the same words, so my memory can't be that bad. Now down to one course a year because of her illness and we hope she can continue that—and without a trace of venality, malice, competitiveness, anything like that. While I, I'm saying without pride, can understand why they'd think I'm a pain in the ass sometimes—opinionated, cynical, etcetera. Jokes that fall flat, though at least my aim's right, since I usually just want to get a laugh. Also, my interests, unlike hers, are fairly limited. News, which I read, I don't find interesting to talk about, and I don't like just about any art in any form done today, and not that much either for the past twenty to thirty years. And pop culture, which gets more and more seriously talked about at these dinners, and which means, most of all, the same American and cutesy or American-inspired foreign films everyone seems to go to or rent and some of the so-called better stuff on cable and public TV, I find trite, dumb, crap, cheap, just junk and silly, and I tend to say so, even if I never see cable, and usually with two to three drinks in me on an empty stomach or only with a few hors d'oeuvres, so say it too much and after a while not too clearly, and oh boy does this go over, insidiously insulting their tastes. While she, ever the—though maybe I'm stepping on a few toes here too, because how do you feel about it?" and she said "Basically the same, while Leonard used to like every movie he saw, no matter how bad. It's hard renting a good movie for myself now, and Leonard hasn't the patience to sit through anything on TV but a baseball game every now and then, though I don't think he fully understands them anymore. He even asks me, who knows zilch about the sport, what some guy's doing on first base when he just ran to it from home plate. And if there are any good plays to go to—" and Irv said "Oh, there are some, usually by the same two Englishmen...we've seen them. My mother-in-law, when she was alive, used to buy special wheelchair seats for us when we came to town," and she said "We can't go to them anymore. Can you imagine Leonard, who wrote them and had one done at the Public Theater, he said, or maybe its café, sitting through one now?" and he said "I forgot; I always think of him as just stories and also a bunch of interrelated stories collected into what he'd call a novel. But I want you to know I don't go into this friends-cutting-us-off too deeply with Loretta. Because no matter how I try taking the blame for it—'It's me,' I tell her. 'They think I'm a pill and only used to invite me because I came with you, but I've become too much for them for even that'—she, always polite and diplomatic, continues to—" and Tessie said "Excuse me, but Leonard suddenly needs me," and he said "Of course. Same thing happens to me all the time, almost to the point where people I'm talking to on the phone think I'm faking it to get off the line. I'll call tonight," and she said "No, you call so much, we should call you," and he said "You've more things to do than I. I'll call."

Called that night: "Everything turn out okay?" and she said "In what?" and he said "Leonard this afternoon. You suddenly had to go to him," and she said "It was nothing. Screaming because one of his sneakers came off, and when he couldn't find it he thought it was lost and I'd yell at him because they were an expensive new pair. The sneaker was right there under his foot but not on it. In other words, his foot was squashing the sneaker—and the pair is decrepit, smelly and full of holes. I've been dying to get rid of them and buy him a new pair, but they're so comfortable now he won't give them up for the world. Anyway, he's napping, but I'll tell him you'll call again. If you do, tell him to let me get him new sneakers. Because no matter how often I throw them in the washer, not only to disinfect them but hoping that'll help them fall completely apart, just being in the same room with them can be a Herculean chore."

Another call: "I'd put him on but he says he's too depressed to talk to anyone today. He wrote me a note telling me this—wouldn't even speak. It's the only thing he's written in months, I think, and which I'm sure is part of the cause for his depression. Maybe you'll have better luck speaking to him tomorrow. The best thing about his illness is that he sometimes forgets he has good reasons to be depressed."

Next day: "He's resting. Probably exhausted from pacing around the house all night, bedroom to kitchen to kids' rooms to the large hallway closet and anywhere else with space enough to pace around in. Oops, wrong again, for here he is, storming into the room towards me. Uh-oh, angry. No, his head's shaking and face is smiling, not angry. Now he's trying to grab the phone out of my hand. —I'm talking, Leonard, just a second; you can't get things that way. —He's like a kid sometimes—*you are*, the way you're acting now—has to have it right away. He knows it's you, maybe because you're the only one besides my sister who calls, and I speak differently to her than I do to you. And he's actually talking now, says I've been on too long. 'Okay, it's your nickel,' he just said. You know what he means? —Because I don't get the expression, Leonard. Nickel? Something cheap? This is a cheap phone call? I don't see how if it's long distance. And 'your' meaning what? Irv's? Mine?" and Leonard said away from the phone "If you don't know, you never will, so don't ask, since it's too late and I was or wasn't supposed...no, it's too late and I was too early for you. And if I do explain, funny as it was or wasn't supposed to be....Ah, I don't know myself anymore. I don't even know myself...then what or who or where was I? What I'm saying, trying to say, and not what Max is saying about know thyself, and pay attention and correct me if I make honest mistakes, and I hope you at least got my maximal line, since I don't want you to think I thought it was some guy named Max on the line...What I'm saying—and one too many lines, right?—is if I tell you it won't be funny as it was supposed to be by my just saying it. So: if I tell you what the line meant, it won't be as funny as it was supposed to be. There. Hurray for myself. Finally I got a sentence out, complete and unfragmented, the meaning of what it means I'll leave to other people to decide, because it's too tough for me," and Tessie said "And you deserve your hurray because that was darn good, clear and to the point," and to Irv "You heard it, didn't you? A very clear sentence, and the ones surrounding it weren't bad either. Just knowing it's you on the phone made his speech and thinking clearer and more focused. I should now tell him it's really my sister on the other end, as a little unkind joke to teach him a lesson about grabbing phones, but it wouldn't be fair to her. Look, he's laughing. He caught on, got the joke. That's good too. —Here, take it, sweetheart.—Speak to you soon, I hope. And you know I'm only kidding about most of the things I said about him. I have to play around with him or I'd die." "Hello," Leonard said on the phone, and Irv said "Leonard, hi, it's me, how you doing?" "I knew it was you. Something told me. I could tell. And don't believe anything she tells you. Everyone's a congenital liar. About this, about that. This, that and that other thing. You know what that was. Not 'liar.' We all know what that is. Everyone is, so they know. But that other. Can't even remember it now it's so big. Too big to fit in my mouth and spit out." "Do you mean 'congenital'?" "I mean it sounded good at the time—not delicious, just good. It made me seem with it and in it and at it and above it and one of the boys and part of the intelligentsia or whatever's the word. A congenital waiter turned writer who drinks continental water. The usual route, which I skipped getting into it because my dad had a little dough. But I was never one for big words. You were." "Me? What are you talking about? I only use them when they're appropriate, because I always go for the shortest, easiest word," and Leonard said "I could never understand half your work. It was good, people said so. Those who were supposed to know, but who knew what they were saying half the time? Too big for my small brain. Do you mind my saying this? You do, I'll stop. You're a nice guy and been a good friend and I don't want to offend anything by saying them to you." "Nah, say ahead. It's good just that we're talking. I don't quite know what you're saying, but that's okay; maybe I'll figure it out later," and Leonard said "Say ahead? Full speed and Moby-Dick. Say ahead! What language you speaking? Isn't English, is it? If it is, I'm lost. I'm serious; it's English?" and Irv said "English, all English. Every now and then I throw in a

French or German or Yiddish word or expression—you used to know more Yiddish than me—but none so far today." "I knew Hebrew, Hebrew. Took it in special Hebrew school, Ben something or another, to the eighth grade. Nine to five, except Fridays; skullcaps and teachers with frisky fists and stinky breath. Why did they all have to eat pickled herring? I liked it too but only on Sundays with seeded rye or bagels. You like all kinds of mixed fish and bagels: onion, poppyseed, cinnamon raisin. You're crazy. Untoasted plain's the only kind, freshly laid. Then in regular high school where I even took the Regents on it and didn't fail. I knew Hebrew, Hebrew, but now I don't know a word but *shalom*," and he hung up. Irv called right back. "What was going on there?" Tessie said, and Irv said "I don't know; he hung up on me. Does he look unhappy?" and she said "No, smiling, when he hung up and now when he wants me to hand the phone to him. Knows it's you again. All right?" and he said "Sure." "Hello?" Leonard said, and Irv said "Leonard, hi, it's me again, what's going on? You hung up on me," and Leonard said "No, when? Ten years ago? Not today; I sneezed. Next thing I know, phone's dead and buried. You brought it back to life. Writer as God again. You must have hung up on me." "Okay, anything you say. So where were we?" and Leonard said "It's good hearing you. Always is. You stick with it. Always have. I did but can't because of whatever I got. Not like all my what friends again? Consistent?" "Congenital?" "You're continental. Everything including the Thomas Mann cap. You told me about that. Or maybe you wrote it. How you or your stand-in wore it overseas while hitchhiking with his work. I find him too smart and stiff. Another great writer, obviously, who I can't read. Has all the qualities critics seek, plus going slow and blowing hard from his crow's neck." "Nah, he was a good man and a fine writer, a little slow at times, true, but you once said he was one of your favorites, especially the short stories." "You always liked guys like that. All the adulterated bagels, while I only liked plain. You also liked them toasted and with lettuce and tomato and smoked turkey on them and mustard of all things, while I can only put on butter or cream cheese. I actually like continental and would have liked to wear that kind of crap. English and *drek* and other languages I don't speak. A continental guy who drinks congenial waters. That's you all over. While Tessie, a continental liar. Don't believe anything she says about me. I've heard. She means well and is a terrific kid—could I be any luckier? But likes to exaggerate to make me feel better. She gives me showers; does yours? I'm done for, though, and the truth is, so are we." "You mean you and I?" and Leonard said "You, me. We're old, out of tune, though you've a few years yet to catch up on me. No longer ripe enough for this page and what we do is all torn up. Like she complains I'm messing up the house and causing a riot with the kids and running over cars and sitting on the cat and jumping on the moon till it snaps and sending the pieces to the French cleaners and which can't come back in one cheese because it's not sliced tripe. Or it is, but how would I know? I'm out of the loop. I miss things that go around, though, but most I don't witness or can't seem to comprehend. How's that for a cap? How's your wife?" and Irv said "Fine, thanks, and thanks for asking. You know, she's got her—" "I hate people who ask but don't actually care. 'How's it going, Leonard?' but what's an answer mean when they have their lives and are entitled to it. I'm miserable, what do you think, but thanks for asking. What's her name again?" and Irv said "My wife's? Loretta." "You don't mind that I forgot? It's a sweet name, ideal for her, her voice and face and smile, a doll. She's like a deer, I remember thinking once. Graceful and soft and other deer-like things." "I remember you saying that too, when you first met her, but calling her a doe." "Did I? What's a doe? Has to be the girl but sounds like the guy. I came to your wedding. Now that was dough, the party. You didn't want too many people at the ceremony." "It was at our small New York apartment, that's why. So just immediate family and the bridesmaid, who was my wife's best friend." "I was your good friend also, I thought, but I won't take it that way. I shouldn't. And I remember a big hall, no apartment. Waiters, tuxes, sit-down tables. Where'd I rent one? I bet I came in my old bar mitzvah suit, embarrassing you." "Believe me, it was at our apartment. You wore a sport jacket. I've photos. Loretta and I did most of the cooking. Long table with food and booze and champagne, and everyone just helped himself. Forty people at the most." "A little band playing Jewish music, I remember." "Are you kidding? A pianist friend of Loretta's who played Bach and Scarlatti." "I remember a clarinetist and a comedian telling dirty marriage jokes. I didn't bring a gift, I bet, and not because I'm cheap." "You gave our first daughter when she was born her favorite book of all time." "She must have been a very early reader." "That's very funny; you're in good form." "I am? I was? I don't get it, though. Better when you don't know you're making them, I guess. Write it down for me so I can repeat it. Or put it in a book, where it'll last longer if it gets good reviews and honorable mention and won't get lost like a note will. Tessie wants me to get off. Says my doctor's supposed to call now. Hell with him. What do I have a doctor for? They tell me to open my mouth. They tell me to follow the pencil. But they're not stopping me from losing my stupid mind and fucking up my family. I should see a mystic instead, for all I get out of them. —I know, I know. —I gotta go, Tessie says so and she's mad at me for what I said about the doctors." "I'll call you back later then, or tomorrow." "What kind of book was that again, the one your daughter was born with?" "A go-to-sleep-if-I-read-you-this-book book. About a mouse in a house and a bear in a chair and a snail on a stairwell and a little girl—or she was a boy, with the physical characteristics of each, so maybe the publisher was pitching it to both sexes and androgynes—who didn't believe in any of it." "Didn't believe what?" "That there was a mouse in the house and bear in a chair and bird in a turd—I forget, really, but I remember she was in pajamas the whole time and pretty surly and skeptical for a kids'-book kid and that the narrator kept saying 'You don't believe? That there's a lion who irons?' and so forth. I must have read it to her a hundred times." "I probably just asked the salesgirl for a good book for a smart kid and she gave me it, but thanks for asking. Ask me where I am, though, and I'll tell you. I don't know. It's my home or one away from one. —Where are we, home?" and Tessie said close to the phone "Come on, Leonard, don't pretend; it's bad enough," and he said to Irv "She thinks I'm pretending. I hope I am. And I'll remember your wife's name again if we stay on long enough," and Irv gave it and Leonard said "You sure? Doesn't sound right. Is this a test? Two and two and two make three. Boy, she's had it rough. Am I right or was that your first beautiful wife?" "She's my first. You must mean—" and Leonard said "Those wide green eyes, your wife's. Like the Homer. Ha, you didn't think me still literary. You're lucky to have someone to take care of like that, because I'm no picnic. Ask Tessie. She wants me off now because of what I might say. She also says I've wasted enough of your money and wants to get me to the bathroom before I make a mess. I told you about her. Always wants me to look sharp and be a straight shooter. You always bring out the yaks in me, even when they're not. But I should go from wherever I am, home or phone. Calls tire me after a while and give me the runs. Write if you don't call. I like your letters better because I don't have to answer them and I can listen without getting up. I don't read myself anymore. Tessie does it for me and likes them as much. You're... you're what? Go on, help me." "I don't know. What are you saying?" "You're asking me? The funny one, I think, so keep them coming. Better than the serious stuff, which you're good but not as good at and getting hard for me to take in." "You're actually the funny guy. Just recently, things haven't been—" "You see? Serious. Knock it off, I don't want to hear that junk. So we're both funny. So we both say nice things about the other. So big deal. What's it got us but flops. Case closed or open and shut. But leave them puzzled. That's what you also do and I stayed clear of because the pants didn't press. That's okay, I guess, but with writing, don't stop. Me?—you're excused," and he hung up.

"What do you think he means?" Irv said to his wife after the call, and repeated the last remarks. "What did he say just before that?" and he said "Plenty, most of which I won't even attempt to remember, what with my atrocious memory for quotes, though some of it, made more sense and he spoke more coherently than he had for months." "So, that's nice for you and hopeful for him. And maybe that last part, because he got tired and faded back to his old pattern, can't stand much unscrambling." "But you're the lit scholar; trained and everything. You can see through words and intentions of what people say much better than I. Let me say them again, but more accurately...I have them here somewhere," and got the paper he'd written Leonard's last remarks on while talking to him, and read them to her. "Not much different than what you quoted from memory. Seems he's saying he's no longer a writer; because of his illness, incapable of being one and maybe ever again. And is also more reader than talker and would rather have what you say on paper so he could make greater sense of it," and he said "Tessie's said whenever she rereads him one of my letters it's as if he's hearing it for the first time, and this can be four to five times." "That's good too. So you write them because he likes having them read to him and you keep them funny and light and forget about everything else." "Just writing to be funny isn't easy for me. There's got to be some context, or whatever's the word. Incident, scene. And to be conscious that there has to be some context, rather than just writing off the top of my head for the fun of it, is—" and she said "Listen, it's obvious something's worked if you say, as you have, that she likes reading them too," and he said "Maybe once she might like them, and not all of them, but four to five times? Some of them were long letters, so what could be more boring for her?" and she said "But there's the added benefit, to balance out the possible tedium of her reading the same letter repeatedly, that someone's writing things to Leonard that interest him. Or at least divert him, make him laugh, and occupy his time in a different way than the usual things he does—eating, TV, having sort of slower prose read to him, sitting outside or by the window and watching the passing planes and birds and cars—and maybe even engage his mind, spark it, if only for a few seconds." "You know, I just thought that she could be saying she likes my letters simply to get me to continue to write them, not that I'd hold that against her. Okay. If I did it before I can probably do it again, though I don't want to spend too much time on it, having so little for my other writing. So I'll try, because it shouldn't only be her responsibility to make the guy laugh, right? And at last an eager and appreciative audience for my work. I'll just have to get in the same writing mood as before. That means typing the things that flit through my head but with the lever in my brain turned on to be cheerful and funny. This could be the first time I give you something of mine to read before it's published, other than for those single lines and phrases here and there when they don't seem right in some way or I feel I'm not being clear. But this time only to make sure nothing's in it that could hurt him or make him angry or sad or more confused. That could be misconstrued, even by Tessie, and end up making one or the other of them feel worse than they already do." "You never know what's going to make someone angry. Especially a very sick person who must have a lot of hidden grievances because he is so sick, even to a good friend like you just because you're healthy. Anyway, I'm sure you'll be safe in what you write, though I'll be glad to look at it if you think I can help."

"Dear Leonard: Actually, 'Dear Leonard and Tessie,' for if Tessie's reading these letters to you, shouldn't they be addressed to her too? But which one of you first? 'Dear

Leonard and Tessie' or 'Dear Tessie and Leonard'? Truth is, now that I've had a chance to think about it, it should be 'Leonard and Tessie' for no other reason than it sounds better that way, like 'Mutt and Jeff' instead of 'Jeff and Mutt,' and 'Abercrombie and Fitch' instead of 'Taylor and Lord,' etc. That said, and a waste of your time, I'm sure, I'm writing you from our place in New York. I know I said I'd drive up to see you next time I get in, but we had massive trouble with the van and it's now being fixed and won't be ready till the day we leave. Should I go into it? It might be pretty dull and will take some explaining at first. Van's been converted, as you know. It was a regular Dodge Grand Caravan and it's now a born-again pain in the ass. I was going to say 'It's now Jewish,' since in these kinds of jokes it's always 'Jewish,' but that wouldn't have made as much sense and would have been a flat joke, which the van, as you'll find out, eventually became. The van in its conversion had its floor lowered, ramp and about 600 lbs. of metal added, and as a result instead of shocks for a suspension system it has air sleeves behind the rear wheels. These sleeves are commonly called air bags, but when I refer to them as that people not familiar with them wonder why our air bags are under the van rather than in the steering column and dashboard. 'How would they help in a collision there?' I've been asked. This van has caused almost nothing but trouble since we got it new two years ago. When it's running well Loretta loves it (I can never love it because I'm always waiting for the next misfortune to take place), since it allows her to be wheeled into the van rather than lifted or thrown in by me, and to sit back in the reclining position of her wheelchair and nap comfortably during the longer rides. But this time, approaching the Lincoln Tunnel on the New Jersey Turnpike, was our worst van incident yet. (Before it was just brakes, axle, steering, electricity, computer, but nothing that couldn't be fixed by most service stations at our leisure and while I rented another car.) The air sleeves went. Or one went, and when one does, the other deflates too. (Same line? Take my air sleeves; please, take my airsleeves!) So, coasting along at about 70, wondering out loud to my family if I'd made the right choice of the tunnel over the George Washington Bridge at this weekday hour (4 P.M.), we suddenly began bouncing up and down as if the van had hiccups or we were on some wild carnival ride that was about to desert the tracks. I slowed down to 20 and now the van's bottom was scraping the pavement and I could hear pieces of van falling off and tinkling down the road. Parked on the shoulder, cars and trucks zipping and roaring past, I checked the air pressure of the sleeves and it was down to 10 lbs. and no doubt sinking fast to ground zero, when at the start of the trip it was an ideal 76 (anything below 50 and the van starts hitting up against the higher bumps on the road). I went a bit nuts and scared everyone in the van including the two usually imperturbable cats. I banged the van roof with my hands and yelled 'Goddamnit' (and worse), 'why the hell does everything have to…' and so on, grabbing the little hair I've left on top and wanting to yank it out and then thinking better of it—I never wanted to be as bald as my dad but I'm getting awfully close and didn't want to accelerate it—and pulled the irreducible sides instead. Showed presence of mind or absence of hair? Isn't it something, though? You look back—I do—and it's a good story now (at least I think so) because the problem's getting resolved and you almost get optimistic that the van's got all its serious troubles and kinks out of the way and from now on it'll run relatively well like most routinely serviced American cars, but when it's happening you feel helpless and don't know what to do because you never faced the problem before and it's also an unbearably hot and humid day. Thank God for my younger daughter (older one's working in a summer camp) who left the van (I can only imagine her initial fright when she saw me screaming and banging and yanking my hair) and patted my shoulder and rubbed my hand (Loretta couldn't because she was in her wheelchair strapped to the floor) and said 'Calm down, Daddy, it'll be okay. Just do what I do when something really bad like this happens. Hold your breath to the count of sixty and then start thinking how to make things right.' I knew I had to do something like what she said or I'd scare them even worse and upset Loretta more than she already was, for she had to know from my angry sidelong glances that I was also cursing her under my breath for having convinced me to buy this overpriced sliced-down-the-middle-and-then-rewelded accursed car. So I bit my cheeks and gritted my teeth and kissed Jackie's head and waved good-naturedly to Loretta and started thinking how to get us out of this spot. 'Let's go,' I said a minute later, mostly because it was too damn hot to stand outside, and we got back in. Once I found that none of the New Jersey repair and tire places we went to could fix the van and most didn't have a clue what to do and that the Arizona chophouse that converted the van was closed because of some state holiday—Canadian Independence Day, very likely—and that its authorized dealer in D.C.—the closest to our Baltimore base and which had serviced the handicapped part of the van a few weeks before—'Check out and fix everything,' I told them, 'whatever it costs. Better that than getting stuck in the heart of nowhere with the one garage there having no idea what to do about the problem'—was closed because it was now past 6 P.M. I drove into the city and up the West Side Highway at 10 mph, cars behind us, especially in the Holland Tunnel which we ended up at, honking the whole way. Put a few dents and holes in the muffler during the trip but I at least got Loretta to our cool apartment and the cats to their litter box. Parked in front of our building (My lucky day! I thought; a spot good for tomorrow), unloaded the van, and at a local Kinko's Jackie went online and found a shop in Bethpage, Long Island that works on converted vans, and ours was towed there the next day. It'll cost a fortune to fix and for the towing (my AAA membership only allowed three free towing miles, and they were too savvy to let me, after I hung up and tried a different agent, upgrade my membership for another $20 to get

100 free towing miles). But the van's being fixed and I hope will be in good enough shape to get us back to Baltimore and maybe even to Maine in two weeks. Anyway, so much inane stuff about us, and once again, unlike Leonard always was in his letter writing, I couldn't be brief. What about you? Anything inane happen recently? I hope things are going reasonably well, and the doctors are coming closer to getting you out of your goddamn lousy rotten situation. I wish there was something more I could do for you than futilely trying to amuse you. Me, I'm still having trouble getting my year-old novel published but am loving the summer break from school. No more manuscripts to read and bad grades to give but my own. Loretta's the same, maybe a bit worse, but it's always up and down with her, though each time losing some. My own health? But what am I talking about? I'm always making things seem worse than they are to heighten the story. She's better than she was a year ago because of the new treatment she's on. I'm feeling okay other than for my gallbladder. Worse pain I ever went through when I had the attack last month other than for Loretta's difficult first childbirth. And I'm including earaches as a pre-penicillin kid that lasted entire nights and the time in my teens an ear-throat-nose and heartless doctor squeezed my infected tonsils with forceps to get the pus out. Was he nuts? A sadist? Was I going to stick around longer to find out for sure? I think he was another of those freebies, which backfired, that my dentist dad arranged in exchange for

his own questionable services on that guy's kids, but after I squirmed out of his grip and off the chair, I bolted for the door. 'Is anything wrong?' I remember the receptionist saying as I ran past her, clutching my throat. This time I thought I was dying, but because of the location of the pain I knew it wasn't my heart, appendix, tonsils or gastric reflux. The pain disappeared in four hours and hasn't come back, but I'm on my guard with poison tablets if it does return with the same intensity. Turned out to be a gallstone stuck in the liver duct, so in a few days I have to have the whole hive removed. All right, I've tried your eyes and, if Tessie's still reading this, her vocal cords, not to say your intelligence, long enough. Hope to see you next time I'm in if I survive the operation (foul-ups have been known to happen), several ounces lighter from the loss of those stones. If I don't see you it'll mean my convalescence took longer than the surgeon said it would—'You'll be eating pepperoni pizza by evening'—and we'll be driving to Maine with no stopover in New York. But what is it with doctors and humor? They try but can't seem to make it. Just looking at me during his two-minute examination, with that big fat book under my arm, he didn't think 'Him? Pepperoni? Even pizza? And in the evening? With what kind of wine?' Anyway, as always, best to you both. Your old pal, Irv."

"Dear Leonard and Tessie: Oh boy, what a trip up. We're in Maine now when for a while I didn't know if we'd ever get here or if I'd even make it to the Garden State Parkway alive.

The van? Why do you ask? Fine for the time being but I'm sure there'll be trouble. My body? Better, but two days ago not so hot. About a week after my gallbladder operation and a tougher recuperation than I was led to expect—if I did like pepperoni pizza (re last letter) I wouldn't have been able to eat it for a week—I was strapping Loretta's wheelchair to the floor (she was in it, van was packed, Jackie in the front passenger seat, cats in the carrier in back) in preparation for the first leg of our trip—Boston. I'd reserved a hotel room for the night for us and the cats, whom we'd sneak into the room in their carrier inside a huge duffel bag on Loretta's lap, supposedly filled—if someone on the hotel staff asked—with her medical and hygienic supplies. But I stumbled (we're back to me on my knees strapping down the chair before setting off from Baltimore) and fell on one of the chair brake handles at the spot where my gallbladder had been removed. Pain was intense for a minute, sort of like getting stabbed with a knife, or once I realized I'd been stabbed, which did happen to me once: while I was a waiter in a mid-Manhattan restaurant shortly before I met Leonard. The cashier was being robbed. This is a true story, not heightened for effect, or I'll try not to make it be, and one I don't remember telling either of you. From my work station about 20 feet away I saw the cashier look in terror at something a man was holding out to her wrapped in a newspaper. (Turned out to be that day's *New York Post*; he dropped it when he lunged at me with the knife. If this were a lousy novel or equally lousy short story I'd make up a dramatic or ironic headline for the paper. THIEVES TAKING OVER NEW YORK. Or CRIME RATE'S NEVER BEEN LOWER MAYOR SAYS.) She was a recent immigrant from Cambodia—this is relevant: her poor English and familiarity with and fear of terror under the Khmer Rouge. I immediately thought, because of her look and that she wasn't busying about the cashier's stand which she usually did when she wasn't taking checks and that he was just staring at her, not saying anything, keeping that rolled-up paper raised: 'Gun, robbery; I got to help her because her English is so bad and in her fear and confusion she might say the wrong thing or scream and get killed,' and that the best way to help her was to casually walk to her stand as if I were taking a customer's check to her—I'd even call out her name, which I knew then and the correct pronunciation of it, and say 'Take care of this please? It's with a credit card,' which wasn't as common a way to pay then, especially not in this upscale burger and brew place—and then chop down on the guy's wrist if I saw a gun in the newspaper and it wasn't pointing at me. I didn't think lots of things: the gun could go off after or while I chopped down on his wrist and put a bullet in me or the cashier or a customer. The robber could shoot me before I chopped down on him. I could chop down on him and miss and then he could aim at me from up close and shoot. I could chop down on his wrist and hit it but not knock the gun away and he could shoot me and the cashier and run out the door 10 feet away. I could chop down on him and knock the gun out of his hand but he could have another gun on him and shoot me. I could get shot in the spine and become paralyzed for life. Or in the head and be a basket case for life. Or shot in the groin and finished there too. Or in the gallbladder, saving me from the worst pain in my life 30 years later—though thinking about it, the tonsil squeezing pain had to be as bad and was probably worse the first minute—and also saving me from the surgery and recuperation after. Though of course getting shot there or any of the other places would have involved extensive surgery and recuperation, so what am I talking about? And if he did have a gun and shot me in two or three places? But I did go over to the stand with the chopping action in mind if I saw a gun in the guy's newspaper, and saw a knife, its tip sticking out an inch. Instead of chopping down on him, or backing away and yelling for someone to call the cops and for the cashier to run, I grabbed him by the wrist and forearm. He hadn't turned to me till then, probably because he hadn't heard me coming—the restaurant's recorded background music was always pretty loud, if I remember, as was the noise level from the tables, since the ceiling was fairly high. He didn't see or hear me also, I think, because he was so focused on the frozen terror-stricken cashier and maybe what he was going to do next to get her to open the cash register, and I also hadn't called out her name and said that business about the credit card and customer's check. My new plan was to either shake the knife out of his hand—again, I did think this and quickly changed tactics—or twist his arm behind his back till he dropped it or his arm broke. I was capable of doing that then and I think I still could if the situation was desperate enough, maybe not for the cashier anymore but for one of my family. But he spun around the second I grabbed him—I was a lot bigger than him, taller and because he was slightly built, seemingly stronger—and threw off my hands and jumped at me with the knife, aiming for my face or neck but getting me in the shoulder. I grabbed his neck with one hand—not the one with the knife in it at the shoulder, and I don't know how I was able to do this and why I wasn't feeling the knife in me yet. Adrenaline; call it what you will. What heroics will do for you; I wanted to save the girl and subdue the brute and maybe get a nice reward from the restaurant and lots of praise for stopping the robbery, but this is what some customers and the cashier and another waiter said I did: tried to strangle the guy with one hand. But he pushed me away, pulled the knife out of my shoulder and ran for the door, though I still wasn't finished with him or feeling any pain. I thought of chasing him—I did; I thought this. Instead, I grabbed the check spear off the stand—you remember, the scary pointed thing the cashier spears paid checks on and when you look at it you often think you're going to accidentally stick your palm through—to throw at him, when the pain hit me for a loop. I'd grabbed it with my good hand, meaning the right one, the side he got me on, and screamed so loud when I went into the motion to throw it that I understand people walking past the restaurant heard me through the closed windows and door. It was dead winter, freezing out, snow in the air but not on the ground yet, meaning snow floating but not sticking, and the door was a revolving one, so it wasn't that they heard me because the door was open when the guy ran out. I was told to sit down. Then to stand with my arm raised, since I was bleeding badly and one of the waiters, who was an actor now but in college had been pre-med, said the raised-arm standing position was the best way to stop me from bleeding so fast till he figured out where to put the tourniquet. I was in too much pain to do anything anyone wanted me to, especially standing now and raising my arm, so some people stood me up and kept me standing but at my first scream they stopped trying to raise my arm. Then they lay me on the floor because someone said that was the best position to stop the bleeding, but with my legs raised. I also had all the other stuff done to me—towels around my shoulder, forehead patted down with a wet rag, someone holding my head up while someone else gave me water, though I hadn't asked for any. They wanted to put a blanket on me but where do you find a blanket in a restaurant, and we only used paper tablecloths. So my own coat was fetched out of my locker downstairs and placed over me. Then EMS came and bandaged me up quickly and gave me something for the pain and put me on a gurney and took me to

Roosevelt. I returned to work a few days later. I knew I wasn't ready yet and so did the manager. But our serving staff wasn't unionized—we'd tried once but were told by the restaurant we'd be laid off if we joined—which meant no disability or sick pay, so I pleaded with the manager to put me back on but with a reduced workload. I was short of dough and the hospital bill was going to cost. I also thought waiting on tables with a bum arm, if I could somehow work it into the chitchat with the customers how it got that way, would get me bigger tips. But since we all pooled our tips, and several of the waiters pocketed a lot of theirs for themselves, I didn't know why I bothered. I had to learn how to write orders and serve with my left hand when my right one hurt too much, and for a few days my co-workers helped me take in my dirty dishes. I did eventually get most of my hospital expenses reimbursed by the restaurant after I wrote a few letters to the company heads requesting it. I'd always been able to write, in that respect, convincingly. I also got a call from the head of personnel for the restaurant chain thanking me for what I did but saying for insurance purposes not to repeat it. They were insured against theft but not so much for death or a permanently disabling or disfiguring injury in stopping a robbery. And as a bonus of sorts, since they didn't give cash rewards because they didn't want to encourage the kind of heroics I did, would I like to train to be a bartender for one of their more high-toned restaurants? I'd make better money and it was a more dignified position for someone my age, he said, since I was about fifteen years older than the other waiters in my restaurant and he'd heard I looked it. I took him up on it and was working at a bar when I met Leonard. Or was I selling clothes in the Little Boys Shop at Bloomingdale's when what's her name, the woman I was seeing then, and who was Manfred's high school English teacher, introduced us? I'm not kidding, I forget her name, but it'll come back to me. Something Russian, though she came from old Huguenot stock on both sides of her family. Tanya? No, though I sometimes called her Volga when she did something distasteful to me like disappear for the night from the apartment we sublet for 18 months to be with another guy. But this is amazing. We were together for more than four years, lived with each other on and off for three, she got pregnant by me and I wanted us to marry and have the baby and she thought I was bonkers to ask her that and she could never in fifty years, and I'm quoting, love me anywhere near the way I did her. Her daughter's name was Frances. Her ex-husband's was Bill. Her father was Lucius the 3rd. Her best friend's was Claire. Her cat was KZ. I'm reciting all these names to try to remember hers but can't. Frances was a terrific kid who got a near fatal disease while I lived with them but after a year was cured. Claire killed herself when she learned her husband Arthur had propositioned neighborhood adolescent boys and was about to be arrested. Lucius flew to London for a week soon after her mother Ernestine died and came back wearing an ascot and derby and swinging a walking stick and told us this elaborate lie, which we all believed, how he had gone on a tour of Windsor Castle and ended up having a private lunch with the queen. Bill married a Dutch woman named Elsa and they divorced a couple of years after they had twins whose names started with T. KZ came to live with me for a week but I took him back in a day after he clawed my genitals in my sleep. Anyway, I think it was the salesman's job I had when 'Volga' introduced me to Leonard, since the cigarette smoke and late hours and dumb conversations with my customers and their nagging me to cheer them up if not make them laugh, when they weren't wheedling and cadging me for drinks, got to me after a while with the bartending one. I also couldn't have known her before the robbery because an RN I was seeing fairly regularly then used to come to my place to redress the knife wound so I wouldn't have to shell out more for hospital visits. But where was I before I went into all this? Maine, great summer day, dry air, light breeze, soft sun, low seventies temperature and biting-bug count: perfect conditions for hanging wash on the line, which I like doing, and then taking it down and folding it up and stacking it in the laundry basket—all done outdoors, of course, with no manmade structures in sight but our van and rented farmhouse. And something about the pain from my gallbladder operation last month, but what? Oh yeah—I had to go back to the beginning of the letter to find out—knife-stabbing pain in my side from having fallen on a wheelchair brake handle while strapping the chair to the van's floor just before we were going to take off. Got me in the ex-gallbladder spot but the pain soon went away. But kept coming back for most of the trip with the same intensity but longer duration, making me think was I the only man born with two gallbladders, and then the improbability of both of them getting stones within a month? Three times I had to stop at a rest area and lay on my back on the grass there, touching my side the way I thought a faith healer might and mantraing 'Please, pain, please, pain, do what I ask you: go away,' till it did. Loretta and Jackie wanted me to drive to a hospital and if I was unable to, Jackie would call for an ambulance. But it was a scorcher that day and too many delays getting to Maine already and I didn't want to hold up my family even more. So I drove on, tried not to show the pain the rest of the way—more heroics, I guess, but I couldn't imagine what Loretta would do (Jackie would just read while listening to CDs through earphones) and who'd take care of her if I had to spend several hours in Emergency waiting to be treated. And what if I had to be cut open again and resewed? I wouldn't be able to drive for days. Felt okay the last 20 miles to Boston, snuck the cats into the hotel, got Loretta settled in our room after a hard trip for her, for she never once got out of her strapped-down chair. I felt fine that night. Didn't have my usual two vodkas on the rocks in our room after a long drive and shower. We went out to a lively seafood house. I'd made a reservation weeks before, since if you don't reserve that far ahead there can be a two-hour wait, and didn't want to lose it. Is the place really that good? Just the onion rings, for one, are like nothing you've ever tasted. If you get to Boston I'll give you the phone number of the restaurant, and the hotel's pretty reasonable too and only a few blocks away. Easy wheeling distance for us with plenty of curb cuts. I ate light—didn't touch a single onion ring—and shared a carafe of wine with Loretta and even had a couple of spoonfuls of their rich desserts. I was feeling confident by then. So there you have it—two stories: my first knifing and second gallbladder. Actually, in San Francisco 30-plus years ago a panhandler slit my cheek (you probably thought the scar was an extension of my worry lines, since my forehead is filled up) with a razor because I only gave him a dime when he insisted I was good for a quarter. I tried telling him I was broke myself and waiting for my first unemployment insurance check to arrive by mail and that he probably had more dough on him than I did. Smart thing to say? Shouldn't have just walked away? I was even about to snatch the dime back from his open palm and say something like 'Not enough for you? Tough shit.' Again, this is what I was like then and maybe still am a little today. The slice must have been clean and quick because I only knew I'd been slit when I felt something wet running down my neck and under my shirt. By now the bum was putting the touch on a man down the street and I wanted to shout 'Hey, watch out for that guy, he's dangerous,' but the man gave without a fuss and it must have been plenty because the bum smiled and casually walked off. But enough. Next letter will be a shorty, I promise, which should come as a big relief to you, and also not go so far off track. Hope you're both well and your kids and I'll write again soon. Irv."

"Dear Leonard and Tessie: Been a while since I last wrote you. Don't want to hit you with any depressing news, but Loretta's been sicker than usual with among other things a constant low-grade fever because of two infections going at once, something I never heard of, with aches and pains and generally feeling miserable, especially days. This has taken up a lot of my time, not that I'm complaining. I actually feel lucky or privileged or whatever you want to call it that I'm able to help her, if I can say that without sounding self-something or other. But because of it I don't get as much of my own work done as I'd like, which doesn't have to be that much. Leonard knows as well as I that the more time we've put into it, the less time we need to do it, and both of us have been at it for 40 to 45 years. But something tells me, especially when I think how it can take me days to do a page, that what I just said isn't true, at least for me, so forget I said it. And if anyone should be complaining—and why am I bringing this up, except maybe to get away from my literary patter?—it should be Loretta with all her illnesses and with me, since I can be a son of a bitch sometimes when I help her, something my family has successfully kept quiet and which I haven't admitted to anyone but my family before. Why this SOB? For the reason I mentioned above: taking care of her takes away from my own work. But then I've done so much of it—all those years, almost without stop—that what's the difference if I don't do more or I'm slowed down? The difference might be that I still like doing it and see things to do that I haven't done and want to, or see them soon after I finish the last thing I didn't see before I started doing it, and so forth. Nah, I don't like that: too pat-on-my-own-backish. Nor that, which is written too literarily, if there's such a word. I should stay away from such talk or self-examination and such mostly because I never doubt my work more than when I'm talking about it. That the same with you? I've never asked and you never volunteered. Anyway— but I forget what else I was going to say. This letter's getting me nowhere and it must be a chore for you to read and listen to, so I should sign off. Otherwise, we're all well, except for Loretta's infections and depression over them, or 'okay,' I'll say, enjoying the good weather and solitude and being in the country, and I hope things are going well or okay for you too. I'll try to write soon and a letter that's more interesting and not as serious. Your pal, Irv."

"Dear Leonard and Tessie: As you can tell from the postmark—if, like me, you look at those—and I find the stamp in my wallet and the air's not too humid today to prevent me from sticking it on an envelope I have and I can remember your address and zip (address book with my manuscripts is in my shoulder bag under a pile of luggage in the back of the van, at the bottom so it gets stolen last) and then drop it in a Kittery mailbox and you have some idea where that southernmost Maine coastal town is in relation to New York and know that Baltimore's another 200 miles from there—we're a little less than a third of the way home. Normally (last 19 years) we'd stop off at our New York apartment for two nights, which'd make us almost halfway done now with that part of the trip, and I'd be able to see you the next day. But Jackie and her friend, who's been with us a week, convinced Loretta and me to drive straight through tomorrow so they can catch the last day of the Maryland State Fair. Gabrielle, who flew up from her camp job ten days ago, also wants to get back early so she can spend a few days with her Baltimore friends before I drive her north to school. By the way, this'll be brief not just because my previous summer letters have been too long but because I'm writing it by hand and am short of paper. My writing paper's in the same bag with my address book and manuscripts, and the motel we're at only provided our room with three sheets of stationery and no envelope or pen. I could get the three sheets in my daughters' room or even go to the main office for more. But I really only have one incident I want to tell you before I forget it, and if I have to I can use both sides of the sheets. But quick, quick, quick before I run out of paper prefacing this and do have to get more stationery or my bag out of the car. I've been reading a novel that's the best I've gotten 80 pages into in years. I'm excited at finally having such a book and I want to continue reading it every chance I get, like on the beach here while the girls are looking for shells and stones to take home, and tonight while we wait for a restaurant table and in bed before I go to sleep. Okay. So around eleven today, when the van's packed and we're about to get in it and go, I announce 'Last chance, everybody, to get whatever you might've forgotten in the house, for once we're a couple of miles from here we're not going back for anything left behind except maybe the cats. So remember to take the cats!' I made a last check of the house—toilets flushed, gas and water knobs turned off, my manuscript bag in the van—and we left. About 30 miles from the house, near Searsport, I thought 'My book!' and looked on both sides of me, it wasn't there, and said 'Anyone see the book I've been reading the last two days—hardcover, white cover, the title *Sevastopol* in red letters designed to look like Cyrillic script? No? Then I'm sorry but I've left it behind and we gotta go back.' Or I said the last a few minutes after I thought about what to do, consequences, is it worth it?, what'll be an hour and a half lost back and forth, for the roads are all single lane to Searsport, etc. 'But you said,' one of my daughters said, 'we can't go back for anything except—' and I said 'Listen, for once let me do something that just benefits me. Sure, our landlady would send it if asked, even by Priority Mail or Express, but I don't want to wait even a day for it. You know how it is with a book you're really caught up in—I've seen you read them for seven hours straight—and

I know exactly where I left it. An hour ago I even saw it there, on the kitchen table, and told myself "Put it in the van now or you'll forget it." Damn, what a dumb ox I am.' So we drove back. Everyone seemed to take it pretty well once I turned around, though there was silence all the way which only ended when we started off again. I knew I'd have to park by our landlady's house on the main road and run the third of a mile down the dirt road to the farmhouse and then run and walk the way back. You see, driving away from the farmhouse earlier I noticed the van was so heavy with five fully grown people and two fat cats and all the luggage and my manuscripts and Loretta's books and the portable air conditioner she insists we have up there for the very hot days—because of her illness: the heat affects her much worse than it does other people—that the bottom kept scraping the bumps and ruts and dislodged rocks in the road and I was afraid of damaging the muffler. I got the book, rechecked the faucets, toilet and stove—I can't trust my memory on these things—and ran a quarterway up the hill and then just walked fast as I could, for it was already hot out and I was sweating bullets. The landlady was   Oops, I see I already wrote on the other side of page 3; I'll have to get more paper. I'm obviously back. There was no stationery in my daughters' room so I had to go to the main office. The guy there said 'What're you doing with all that paper, writing a book?' I almost said 'You don't know how close to the truth you are with that question,' but the last thing you want to admit to most people is you're a writer. For they usually say—you must have got it plenty of times—even if they've read only five books in the last ten years, which I think is the average for the nation, 'Should I have heard of you? What are some of the titles? You use your real name? Have you ever been condensed?' and then you have to reassure them they haven't missed anything. Our landlady was at the van when I got back and I held up the book, figuring someone had already told her what I'd gone down for, and said 'Now you know me; no effort's too great for literature.' She said 'Why didn't you knock on my door and have me drive you?' and I said 'I didn't want to bother you and I also didn't think of it.' Then I kissed her goodbye again and we drove away. I thought Loretta (we hadn't spoken of it yet) mostly admired what I'd done—nobody would go more out of her way for a book than she, if she could—and that her silence since Searsport wasn't out of sufferance or withheld scorn. Think of her sacrifice in not asking me to drive on and leave the book: an hour and a half more sitting in her wheelchair. I admit I didn't think of that till now. If I had I might have left the book, called the landlady from the first pay phone I saw along the way and asked her to FedEx the book to our New York apartment right away, for that was our destination at the time. But then what would I have done? For you see, it was only when we got to Kittery that the girls begged me to drive straight through to Baltimore tomorrow. They even used my going back for the book as part of their argument: 'You did what you wanted to do, which wasn't easy for us but we understood what it meant to you, so why can't we get something we really want too?' I would have told them I have to pick up the book in our apartment building, so it made no sense not to spend the night there. They would have said we could leave for Baltimore right after I got the book, and Loretta and I would have told them it was too long and exhausting a trip that way, and the cats need a break too. 'How would you feel,' I might have said, 'not eating and drinking and peeing for around twelve hours or stuck in a cage for hours with your own pee and maybe worse?' They would have said we could rest a bit in the apartment before setting off for Baltimore, and the cats could use the litter box and get something to eat and drink then. But I would have insisted we stay. You would have done the same, wouldn't you—go back for the book? You're bookpeople, and what's more important sometimes than a book you're enthralled with and want to read every chance you get? (Just that I got 80 dense pages read in a day and a half during a time I was doing lots of housekeeping and packing and stuff and that I'm a terribly slow reader, says something about the book's hold on me.) But your kids, if they were with you on this hypothetical trip home, are much younger than mine and probably wouldn't be able to take the trip as well. So you wouldn't have gone back for the book, and who could blame you? And in case you're wondering—writers, like detectives and lawyers, are always finding catches in people's stories, which is why I'm trying to cover everything—it wasn't a book I could have bought in a good bookstore along the way. The bookstore owner in the town nearest us gave it to me the other day. Not a particular admirer of this writer's work but knowing I was—I'd bought two of his previous novels, one a hardcover, at her store last summer and talked up the author a lot, which surprised her because I hardly say anything good about anyone's work—she parted with the advanced reader's edition the publisher had sent her. I'm a good customer—my whole family is—so I'm sure she also gave it to me for that. We even order books from her the rest of the year, but only ones we don't need immediately, to throw some business her way when no tourists and summer people are there. Anyway, the book isn't out yet and the cover says it won't be for another two months. If it continues to be so good I'll send it to you when I'm done and you can return it next time I come in and I'm able to see you, which should be in a few weeks. If you can't finish it by then, don't worry; I rarely read a book more than once unless I'm teaching it, and this one I'll never teach, since the students would revolt at reading a 300-page book with only two paragraphs and one period. So that's it, my big incident. It was supposed to deliver more than it did, but significance always eludes me. And not at all brief as I intended it to be and made even harder to read by being handwritten, but it would have been too difficult to extract either of my two type-writers from the van. Now for creative stuff—the first draft of something and which needs speed—I would have unloaded the entire back for one. Okay, I have the envelope, I remember your address, and I'll look in my wallet for the stamp now, which I doubt will be sufficient postage for six sheets of stationery and all that ink. I'll drop it in a mailbox anyway, with yours as the return address on it to increase the odds it gets to you, and hope for the best. Regards from Loretta and I'll write again soon. Irv."

"Dear Leonard and Tessie: Wish I had some real good news for you for a change. We're home and I'm healthy and so are the kids, but that's about it. My new-old manuscript is still being multiply circulated by my agent after a year and gets roundly and squarely but not uniquely rejected. She just sent me a batch of them after I asked, since I hadn't heard from her in six months, if she was actually submitting the work: 'Unfortunately his books have been a poor seller for us and generated little attention and few reviews, so I'm compelled to let this go without a look.' 'It's everything one should expect from an intensely ambitious contemporary novel by a seasoned writer who apparently could never stomach line-by-line editing and considerable cutting, so not for our list.' 'I've never been a fan of his work, but I'm sure some young editor in town is and will do the novel justice and offer a more than generous advance.' 'Dietz's novel seems like a shoved-off rowboat without an oarsman, if you get my drift. As for your second author, Gretchen Gravitas, now here we have a find. I love the unpretentious non–attention-getting style and consistently coherent structure and wise and heartwarming universal theme, and I hope to get the big chief's go-ahead on it by the end of the week.' 'I'm more than likely in the minority on this, but his novel is offputting to totally disengaging, confirming my reluctance to look at it when you first proposed the idea. Please, though, keep me in mind for future work of any of your other more promising clients.' 'If I were sure you'd keep this between us I'd reveal what I truly feel about this novel and the little I've read of his previous published work. But he's reputed to have a sharp temper and to write acrimonious and at times threatening letters to editors who have rejected his work and has even phoned them at home, so I'll hold my tongue. Next week, lunch?' I don't know where the last editor came up with that about me. I never expected to get published even in small magazines and I've more than once told the agency to drop me, as the money they make off my work barely covers the cost of representing it. Anyway, best thing in not getting the novel accepted is it saves me the chore of going over the galleys and before that the 500-page copyedited manuscript and challenging nine out of every ten corrections and crossing out most suggestions and then having reservations and can't-sleep nights about the ones I went along with. About Loretta: she's developed another serious internal infection and antibiotics seem to be helping her but fouling up her digestive tract. Drove Gabrielle to her first year at college. That left a great void in the house but also a free bedroom I can move to when Loretta's making loud breathing noises in her sleep, one sounding like a door screeching open and another like buzz-sawing. She's been doing that most mornings starting around four ever since she fell out of her wheelchair a while back and broke her nose. Had to return to teaching last week, a job I can hardly do anymore. My 22nd year at it and I'm quickly burning out and becoming like most of the teachers I disliked when I was a college student: contemptuous, grumpy, hard to find and unapproachable. Though I love most of my students I now hate all their work and them when they hand it to me, no matter how good it might be. Six years, when Jackie graduates college, till I can retire, though I don't know how I can hold out that long. I just want to read, write, look after my family and attend to the necessary little things, and nap when I feel like it after my immediate obligations to Loretta are done. But what can I do if I'm the only moneymaker here and the kids' college expenses and Loretta's medical and homecare and physical therapy bills (the ones not covered or paid in full by health insurance) are so high? Also, when we got back to Baltimore from Maine we found our house had been burglarized. We pulled into the carport, glad to be home and done with the long drive. I was out first, intending to unlock the front door to the kitchen, throw open a few windows to start airing the place, run down to the basement to turn the water heater control from Vacation to Normal, when I saw there was no door, or rather, it was on the floor along with part of the jamb and wall, and from the opening I could see clear through to Loretta's study and my daughters' bedrooms that the house had been ransacked for the second time in three years. What did they get? Not that much. Two of the three bicycles we had, both brand new, were taken the last time from inside the house, where I'd put them as a precaution against theft, and my old one was stolen from the garden shed this past winter while we all slept. Most of Loretta's jewelry—nothing fancy; family hand-me-downs and a few things she picked up in the Soviet Union years ago and kept in lacquered boxes she also got there and treasured—were stolen in their boxes during the last house burglary, and what she had left and didn't take to Maine she hid in a Tampax box on a bathroom shelf, having been told male thieves would never think of looking in it or have an aversion to sticking their hand inside, afraid they might come up with a used one. Five to six watches my in-laws had given me over the years, none of them used except when my Easy Reader Timex needed a new battery, which usually takes me weeks to replace: one with scissors for hands, another with a choo-choo train that goes around the dial several times on the hour and also, if you have the switch on, toot-toots the hour or just toots if the hour's one; two identical square-faced watches given at different times, with Roman numerals I can't read because they're so small. Cameos my mother got in Bermuda on a cruise she went on a few months after my father died. About a year before she died she gave me them to give to my daughters when they reached sixteen—'If you give them before they might lose them or give them away,' she said, 'and they're quite precious and have become my two favorite pieces and I'd love your girls to always remember me with them.' I forgot who was to get which, something my mother was very specific about, so put off giving Gabrielle hers till I remembered. What else? The bigger items—TV, computers, CD player—weren't touched. Just the stuff they could carry out in their pockets, I suppose, which makes me think the thieves were local kids who came by foot or bike—maybe even our bikes—because they were too young to drive a car. My God, I just realized: my father's pocket watch. It's a half hour later. I looked all over for the watch. I kept it and its platinum fob in the same drawer, one the thieves had dumped on the floor, with the cameos and my hankies and underwear and socks, in a velour bag that once held my small collection of marbles when I was a boy. My mother's dad gave my father the watch as a wedding gift in 1926. It's worth a lot, fob and watch, and there's the sentimental value: other than for several photos of my folks looking very happy and sporty together when they were just dating and a few from before that: my father at the wheel of a roadster and in another rowing a boat, my mother in a bathing suit on a boardwalk, holding a parasol above her, and in another pressing a furry puppy to her cheek—and photos of my kids with Loretta the day they were born and a few others of them together, that was it, the only things I'd really miss if they were gone. And the high school ring of my sister, the one thing I have of hers other than for a few photos of her when she was well, so those too. I know I told you of her but only in passing. Leonard and I hardly ever spoke much about, what do you call them?—our first families, except for some good stories of our folks, all of them turning up in our work. The ring is always on the windowsill in front of my work table where I'm writing this. I'm sure the thieves if they saw it knew it wasn't anything they could sell or wear. The watch, though, I always took to Maine with me, as a safe-guard against it being stolen if the house were broken into. So why'd I forget it this year? My mind again. Works okay some-times, other times it's a bust. Also leaving the cameos, but they weren't nearly as valuable as the watch. My mother gave me it after my father died. Said to sell it if I needed the money. 'If you don't sell it,' she said, 'you'll likely lose it, knowing how you forget things. It's a Howard. They were very expensive even back then, and my father was no cheapskate and only bought, unlike Dad'—this was the only thing she was hard on my father about and made these comparisons—'the very best.' But I never would have sold it. After it being in the family for around 50 years, probably 45 of them in their bank vault, since she said he never wore it after the first few years of their marriage—it was too old fashioned for him—it wouldn't have seemed right someone else having it. So what would I have done with it? My daughters never expressed any interest when I showed them it, though the chain they liked. I should have given it to my brother long ago, since I knew I'd lose it eventually. The watch was 'lost' or 'stolen' or 'bamboozled' in a number of pieces of mine, mainly, I think, to prime myself for the loss of it when it really did disappear. My brother's much more careful with valuable things than I and could have passed it on to his son. So why'd she give it to me and not him? She said because of all the help I gave her with my dad. Turning him over in bed every night and giving him injections, taking him for walks in his wheelchair…it's funny how prepared I was for Loretta's illness. Changing him some nights when I came in to turn him over and he'd had one of his frequent accidents. Now I won't even tell my brother the watch was stolen unless he asks if I still have it. He won't give me hell but he will say that if I didn't think I could be more careful with it I should have given it to him to keep in his bank safe till I wanted to sell or repair it or something, since in a way I'd been entrusted with it. The watch didn't work and I don't think it ever will for more than a few days for whoever ends up with it now and gets it fixed. The two times I did it stopped running shortly after. Oh, so much stuff about the watch. After I finish this letter I'll have to call the policewoman in charge of the burglary case, which means looking for her name and the report number when I thought I was done with the whole thing. And then our home insurance company. I'm sure that'll entail my going to a watchmaker, if any still exist around here, to get an estimate as to how much the watch would be worth. When I first got it almost 30 years ago the watchmaker offered me $500 for it. Actually, I don't think I'll contact the insurance company any further. Does this sound like the dumbest idea or wrongheaded principled notion going, but why should they have to pay for my negligence or just lousy memory? The broken door was another matter; I did lock it and also set up several light timers around the house and taped a warning on both entry doors that the house was protected by pet rattlesnakes so if you break and enter come equipped with anti-snake bite medicine. But if I call the policewoman, maybe there's a way to get the watch back. It's possible she's in contact with all the pawnshops in the area or any place a watch like that might be brought. But no shop or the present owner who bought the watch from the shop's going to give it up so easily after they paid what could be a bundle for it unless I had absolute proof it was mine. Unlike my sister's ring, there's no inscription on it (hers had her three initials on the inside of the band, another reason no thief would steal it). It's just a pocket watch with a platinum silver chain. The chain might even have been removed, sold separately or given to the thief's teenage girlfriend or daughter. The watch, of course, had 'Howard' on its face, that's all I remember, and a silver back that opened. No, I know more. I described parts of it in those pieces I wrote about it getting stolen or lost, so I'll have to go back to them, something I hate doing with my old published stuff. Though when you think of it, something useful might finally come out of my work. Sorry for ending on so sorry a note and in such a sloppy hurry, but right now contacting the policewoman and trying to find what's got to be the most precious and valuable thing I own takes precedence over everything else. Speak and write to you soon. Irv."

"Dear Tessie: Tough to know where to begin. It's been a harrowing month, I'll start off with, which is why you haven't heard from me. And I'm addressing this letter only to you with the hope you'll read it to yourself first, as a lot of what I'll be writing in it might not be good for Leonard to hear, though you be the judge. About a hospital and Loretta being very sick in it because of a medication screwup, something Leonard once went through but at home, and where for a few hours I thought she might die. Leonard could imagine the same thing happening to him in the health care center, as you call it, he's in, and use it as a reason to pressure you to take him home, which you said in your last letter he's in no condition to. Anyway, here goes, though a couple of far less dramatic things first. I never found my dad's pocket watch. I gave the policewoman, if you remember, a good description of it based on several passages in my fiction, but the watch was nowhere in the area, she said after checking, or nobody was admitting he had it. Kids are well, I am too, and Gabrielle loves college. But Loretta more than a month ago suddenly had to go in for another operation. You might recall the first one almost two years ago. A computerized pump was inserted right above her stomach. It regulates the most important medicine she takes—I can't spell it so won't try—and it stopped working and was causing problems—legs shaking like crazy or tree-branch stiff and sometimes panfully so for both those and it was impossible to set her comfortably in bed or in her wheelchair—so the pump and some of its tubing had to be replaced. The operation went smoothly and she was fine when she came out of the anaesthesia in ICU. Smiling, cheery, not groggy or in any pain. I was there only a few minutes—all they'd allow me. Then stayed with her in her hospital room till closing, when I was relieved by a private nurse. Though the nurse cost plenty and we had the same one for eight straight nights—sorry if I sound like my dad there, but for a while before I hired her I did think of the expense—it was supposed to be money well spent. Fewer nurses on the floor at night, so a private nurse or nurse's aide (I actually think that's what hers was, which, to be honest, cost ten dollars an hour less than an RN but we were told an aide was all she'd need) could summon a hospital nurse if Loretta was in any immediate danger or needed something done for her that a private nurse or aide wasn't able or allowed to do. I called Loretta at seven the next morning, knowing she'd be up because of how busy hospital floors are at that time. She said she was okay, they'd got her pump going a few minutes before and it seems to be working fine, and she was a little tired—probably the aftereffects, she said, of the anaesthesia and painkillers and being woken up at six to take pills—and was going to nap, so I should hold off coming till noon so she could get a long rest. The private aide's shift ended at nine but Loretta said there were plenty of nurses looking in on her during the day and she was also hooked up to machines and being monitored from the nurses' station. I got to her room around eleven, just in case she was up. She was fast asleep. Phone rang several times—her dad, friends—but she didn't even stir. When I said to her at noon 'Not time to get up now? Your lunch is here and you've been asleep for five hours,' no response. I shook her a little; nothing. Felt her forehead and cheeks and chest; no sweat or fever or unusually cold skin, but I thought just touching her like that would at least make her open her eyes. The television above the other bed in the room was loud and grating—some stupid talk show—but that didn't wake her either. And the other patient in the room, when I told her something didn't seem right with my wife—she's sleeping too soundly, doesn't move when spoken to or touched; she's like a zombie with her body rigid and mouth staying open and not even an eye blink—said 'I was also wondering about her. Her phone rang like a dance band before you got here—I had one of the aides turn it down because it was disturbing me so long—and she didn't answer it when I asked her to or make the slightest sign she heard me.' I went to the nurses' station and said to the woman there that something seems wrong with my wife. 'Who's your wife?' she said and I gave her name and she said 'What room?' and I gave it. She checked the monitors at her desk, said everything—pulse, breathing, blood pressure, I don't know, but several of them Loretta was hooked up to—is normal, so she's just sleeping extra peacefully because her body needs it, and I said 'But it's been more than five hours. That's too long for late morning, after she's probably slept all night, wouldn't you think?' and she said 'If any of her vital signs weren't right, I'd say yes.' 'Listen,' I said—I was getting angry—no, I was angry—but knew showing or expressing it would just make her argue back to me, saying something like 'Excuse me, but if you want to get something, you're not going about it the right way,' which would only delay getting help for Loretta—'I'm really worried. You can see it in my face and what I'm saying, can't you? So please have a doctor or nurse look at her right away?' and she said 'Okay, that can be done. Let's see who's covering that corridor,' and looked at a work schedule sheet and called out to one of the nurses sitting at the station 'Felicia, would you check on Mrs. Dietz in 22A?' Felicia held up a finger: one minute, and went back to the medical chart she was reading. I wanted to say 'Is she kidding? Tell her it's an emergency. I want her to go now,' but I went back to the room. Ten minutes later Felicia still hadn't come. Loretta was the same: same position, mouth open, no sign she could hear anything, though her chest was now heaving, it seemed. I said to her 'Sweetheart, you've been sleeping long enough. Get up, you got to get up, I'm getting scared for you,

very scared. Give me a sign. Please. Say something, open your eyes. Or don't open them, but smile, grab my hand,' and I put my hand in hers; she didn't grab it or even try. I shook her shoulder, scratched the top of her hand, then tried tickling her palm. 'This is ridiculous,' I said to the woman in the next bed. 'You're worried as hell. You tell them it's urgent. You're polite and don't yell but it's written all over your face how you feel about your wife and their goddamn foot-dragging, and still no one comes.' She turned down her television. 'They can be awful, I know. Not all the time—most are very nice—but at night when I need something? It can take hours. Ring for the nurse; that button there,' and I said 'Damn, why didn't I do it sooner? Forgot it was here,' and pressed the button and the woman out front said 'Yes?' and I said 'Felicia never came. It's been more than ten minutes. My wife seems worse. Her chest is heaving, as if she's having trouble breathing, and she still doesn't respond to anything.' 'I'm sorry. She was called away suddenly and I've been trying to get someone else. We're a bit short-staffed today. Someone will be right there. Promise."
'Watch,' the other patient said. A few minutes passed. 'That's it,' I said, and ran to the station. The woman there was on the phone. I said 'Excuse me, but you promised someone would be right there. Would you please get someone to check on my wife right away?' I know I'm going on too long with this and repeating myself in parts. But a lot of it was repeats—over and over asking her to see to Loretta and then asking why nobody

had come and would she get someone right away. I don't know why I included the woman in the next bed. Maybe because her TV was so annoying, which only added to my frustration and in some way my alarm, and that there was someone there watching Loretta dying, I felt, and me going crazy. And sure, the dialogue isn't word for word what I said and heard. But the actions are close, to what happened: waiting, trying to get Loretta to open her eyes and grab my hand and my going back and forth to the station, the last two times running, and now, when the woman held up her hand for me to wait till she was off the phone, I banged my fist on the counter between us and yelled 'I'm not kidding anymore. Get the fuck off the phone and get someone for my wife now. I think she's in serious danger and in a coma. I want a doctor—an emergency team— to go to her in room 22, bed A. Any of you,' I said to the other hospital people at the station, all of them gawking at me of course, 'if anyone here's a doctor or nurse, please go to my wife's room, that's 22A, to help her.' Nobody made a move. The woman put down the phone. 'Who's your wife's doctor?' she said. I said 'What's the difference? Get any doctor who can handle an emergency.' 'No, I'm not making myself clear. What's the name of the physician who admitted her into the hospital for her operation? We'll page him, because all this could be attributable to her condition.' 'Damn,' I said, slapping my head, 'I should have called him a half hour ago. He would have got you people going. It's Dr. Still. But he could be in his

office up the street, or anywhere—at another hospital he's
affiliated with. So just get her any doctor. I think she's in a
coma and dying. So get one,' and I banged the counter again.
'Get one, get one,' bang, bang. 'All right,' she said. 'That isn't
the way to get attention or help from me or anybody on the
staff. But you want a doctor for your wife, I'll call for one, but
first let's quickly get a nurse in. Darlene,' she said to a woman
at the station. 'That's not your corridor, but could you go with
this man to look at his wife while I page the resident and Dr.
Still?' I ran back to the room. Turned around when I got to the
door and Darlene was walking at a normal clip and I said
'Quick, quick, every second could count.' She pulled the
curtains around Loretta's bed, checked the tubes and IV bag,
blood pressure, bandages—okay, she did lots of things and
then said 'All the equipment's working and physically she
checks out fine. It's just a deep sleep she's in.' 'It can't be.
She doesn't respond to anything, noise or touch. Only her
breathing's changed since I was last in here; it isn't as labored.'
Two young doctors walked in. They checked all the things the
nurse had, examined Loretta more thoroughly. One said 'We
can understand your anxiety, but it's what the nurse told you.
Your wife's in no danger, there's nothing to worry about, and
she should come out of her sleep well rested in an hour or two.'
'Can't anyone hear me?' I said. 'She's in a coma. A coma's
when you can't wake someone up. Can you wake her up?' 'Not
quite true,' the other doctor said. 'An extremely deep sleep

or heavily narcotized state can resemble a coma and often manifest—' but I cut her off and said 'She's not on narcotics. She was on a painkiller yesterday but they make her nauseous and constipated, so she took herself off them. And I've tried everything to wake her. Pinching, shaking, pricking. Do it yourself. Use a needle or safety pin or whatever you use. And I'm more than familiar with comas. My parents and sister were all in comas till the last minute of their lives and I was with them when each of them died. Holding my mother's hand through the bed rail. At the foot of my father's bed. He was in a coma for three days when I'm convinced, when the medical team came in and shooed me out of the room, that they took him off life support so he could die. My sister, I don't know— maybe she came out of it at the very end, for her eyes opened. I'd lifted her up from her bed because she was choking on her phlegm, and she died while I held her. Two in hospitals and my mother at home. So I know a coma from a deep sleep and you've got to do something for her before she dies because of what you didn't do.' They told me to calm down, they'd examine her again and if they found her life was being threatened in any way, they'd summon the hospital's emergency team. They examined her and after it, shook their heads, ready to tell me, I was sure, that everything was normal with her, when her main doctor—the specialist—the one who told her to have the operation in this hospital—came in. He smiled and politely said hello to me and stuck out his hand to shake and I said

'Please, no formalities. Just see to her.' 'Trust me. It's one of two or three things and I know what they are and each can be remedied easily.' He examined her with an associate from his clinic, opened a machine that looked like a laptop computer and plugged it into an outlet and extended what seemed like a microphone from the machine to her stomach where the pump was and punched several keys and the screen lit up and displayed lots of lines and columns of letters, numbers and symbols and a few words like her name, his, the hospital's, mine for insurance purposes, and the drug's. 'What I thought it might be,' he said. 'A first, maybe a second for us in these replacements, but definitely the culprit,' and had his associate go to the hospital's pharmacy closet, he called it, for the antidote, since it'd be faster that way than waiting for it to be delivered. While his associate was gone, he held her hand and rubbed and patted it and looked at her most of the time while he explained to me what the problem was: 'Oversupply of her antispacticity drug. A residual amount'—and I know I won't be able to even paraphrase this well; I didn't take notes, of course, nor write any of it down later—'must have been in the pump and which I thought would have been flushed or drained during the operation or else dissipated in her system overnight. Probably not much of it was left but enough, when combined with the drug she was getting after we got the pump started this morning—' But you get the point. Overdose, not oversupply. Sent her into a coma. They were sloppy.

Incompetent. Maybe the surgeon too, whom he was shoving some of the blame on. But this main guy, whom Loretta has a little less confidence in now. But he's so smart, smooth and personable—offered us coffee and croissants in his office first time we saw him, asks us about our kids and always tells us about his, once said he tried buying any one of my books but the store was all sold out. 'Sold out?' I said. 'They never carried any and didn't think it paid to order one for you,' if he really did try, since he also says he's too busy to read anything but medical literature—that I'm sure in a couple of months her confidence in him will be completely restored. But he should have known, since he must have been warned about it in his medical literature, not to have started up the pump with the new drug before he was sure all the old drug was out. And the old drug was pretty old, as the pump hadn't been working for months, so maybe that had something to do with it too. Though he never admitted it was a coma. Closest he came was 'It could have been one, or a profound noncomatose sleep brought on by the additional medication. Too much of it can make you very tired. But if you want to call it a coma, I won't argue with you.' 'Oh, what's the difference now,' I said—this was days later. But we're not through. The associate returned with the antidote. Still administered it and said as he pulled out the needle and wiped alcohol over the entry hole 'This should rouse her soon enough and also diminish all your worries about her. She'll be awake a short while and then sleep peacefully.' She opened her eyes in a few seconds, looked frightened, tried to speak but couldn't get any words out and then seemed to have trouble breathing and said 'Help... help...help...my heart...I can't breathe...I'm dying...help... help...help.....' 'You're fine, dear,' Still said, lying her back because she'd sat up. 'You're breathing without any difficulty whatsoever. It's the medicine we gave you that's making you feel like this, but it's all in your head.' 'What do you mean it's in her head?' I said. 'It's obvious she's having trouble breathing.' 'No,' he said. 'The medicine does that for a short time. It's a jolt to her system—extremely strong stuff, which it'd have to be to do what we ask it to—but she's fine, believe me, she's fine,' while Loretta was sitting up again and saying 'Help...help...breathing...I can't breathe...my system...I'm dying...help me...help me.....' 'You can breathe,' Still said. 'Take it from me, my dear: it's the antidote we gave you—a very strong medicine that's making you feel your breathing is bad. You were sleeping too long. The antidote got you up a little too fast. Now you're fine. Try to think it's only the medicine that's making you feel you can't breathe.' 'I can't breathe...I can't breathe...I'm dying...help me...help...help.....' 'Tell her everything's fine, she's breathing perfectly, it's just the medicine she just got,' he said to me, and I said 'As Dr. Still said—maybe you heard—you're going to be fine, sweetheart; you are fine. If you weren't, there are lots of doctors and nurses in the room to help you. But as you can see, they're not doing anything. They don't have to. They only came in to say hello and see you awake after a long nap, so everything has to be okay with your breathing and heart.' 'Heart…my heart…it hurts…I'm dying…I'm breathing…help, I can't breathe.' One of the young residents said to Still 'Nothing could be wrong. All her lines check out all right, as did the exam we gave her before you got here.' 'I know, that's what I'm saying,' Still said. 'But I don't know how to get that through to her.' His associate, standing by the bed across from Still, said 'Listen to me, Michelle; it's Dr. Moran. (Michelle? Where'd he get Michelle? He'd treated her alone and with Still lots of times, so some other patient's name must have popped into his head. I didn't correct him because I thought that would have made things worse for her: 'They don't even know who I am. They're giving me medicines for someone else.') You say your heart hurts. How does it hurt? Does it feel as if it's pumping too hard? That's the medication we just gave you making you think that, but that feeling will go away. Is there a tightening in your chest that feels as if it's squeezing your heart? Again, it's the new medicine making you think that, and will go away. Because your heart's normal. Better than normal. I should have a heart that's working as well as yours. Same with your lungs—and your whole breathing apparatus: normal and clear.' 'But if she says she's having trouble breathing,' I said, 'and her chest hurts (she was still saying this and calling for help and giving no sign she understood anything we said or recognized any of us, though she stared at me more than she did the others), then maybe something is the matter. Maybe she needs more tests or oxygen or an emergency team in here with resuscitation equipment and such just in case.' 'Don't tell her that,' Still said. 'Oxygen tube in her nose, when she's breathing adequately on her own, would make her more anxious and overstimulated, and we've more than enough staff and equipment in here already. And suggesting something could be wrong with her doesn't help things either. You've seen her. Out of it as she is, she picks up on everything we say and distorts it in her head to something godawful. —You're fine, dear,' he said to her. 'As Dr. Moran said, better than fine. There's nothing to worry about and you'll be sleeping like a baby in a few minutes.' This went on for another half hour. Her not responding to our questions and repeating that business about her breathing and dying and heart hurting and so on. Then she got silent all of a sudden, and her eyes closed and she let me lie her back in bed. She'd kept sitting up through all this till I finally convinced the doctors to let me keep her up, since I thought (they didn't agree with me on this but didn't see the harm, though they never gave me a good reason for keeping her flat) her breathing would be better and pressure in her chest would lessen in an upright position. Still said they'll watch her extra closely the next day but he was positive she wouldn't have any further distress. 'Biggest problem could be, you think you'll ever speak to me again?' and I said 'Why not? Accidents happen and she seems fine now, and he said 'Just kidding. I know you're an easygoing guy who thinks grudges are for petty-minded sluggards and that we're still friends,' and he and Moran shook my hand and left. Scariest time of my life? You bet. Glad I was there? Without question yes. Did I do more harm than good by goading them to jump-start her out of her coma? I'm beginning to think so because of that wake-from-the-dead injection I feel almost caused her death. Do I still trust the docs? No, but would a different doctor team and hospital be any better? I doubt it. Do I worry something like this will happen again when she goes in for another pump replacement, which they say she'll have to do every four to five years? Yes. Did I feel right leaving her every night when the visiting aide came? No. The alternative was getting her a private room at considerable expense and a cot in it for me, at least for a few nights. But I told myself nothing will happen, she's out of danger, if anything goes wrong overnight the aide will phone me. Did I trust the aide would look after her okay? Sort of, even if I was sure she napped most of the time but that if anything went wrong the monitor beepers would go off and wake her. Did I feel guilty not hiring a visiting nurse instead of an aide the first week? Yes. But again I thought of the extra cost and later justified it to Loretta that we knew everything would be all right. Did I think when I was home the first few nights that I might get a call she was in serious distress? Yes. But I still got to sleep without a hitch and in the morning, after I drove Jackie to school and spoke to Loretta and heard she was okay, got a couple of writing hours in. She remembers nothing from that day. Truth is I may photocopy this before I mail it to help me remember that day in case I ever want to write about it. I won't go on about the length of this letter. Longest I've written anyone. Oh, there was one when I was around nine to an uncle on a ship in the Pacific during the war, pages and pages that took me a whole day to write and which he probably dumped, if he got it, after the first one. Who wants to read what a kid has to say unless he's yours? I took Loretta home last week. She's still uncomfortable because of all the cutting and stitching and has trouble finding a good position to sleep in no matter how many pillows I put around her. Anyway, this is why I didn't visit Leonard when I said I would, though I'm excuseless why I haven't written sooner. We'll be in New York the weekend after next. So that Saturday or Sunday, depending if we leave on Friday or Saturday (because Jackie will stay behind to be free of us for a day, we can only spend one night away), I'll come up to see Leonard in that new place in the Bronx he's at. I'll call before to get directions by car, if you know them from the West Side, and also to make sure Leonard's still there. Hope you're all well, and my very best. Irv."

He goes to see him. First, on Pelham Parkway, something seems wrong with the brakes. Can't be, he thinks. I just had the damn things fixed. Tests them a few seconds later when no car's in front or behind him and they seem to work. Tests them again when he's a few hundred feet from a red light, and he has to floor the pedal before the van starts to brake. So what the hell's going on? he thinks. Tries them when he's approaching the next intersection and van comes within inches of hitting a truck waiting at the light. "This car," he says. "This goddamn freaking rotten car. I hate it," and slaps the steering wheel. "Now what do I do? We got to get home today. We have no other way."

Before he left the apartment he got Loretta set in her wheelchair, radio and portable phone on the side table next to her, things she can read, tissues, pen and legal pad, address book, her glasses cleaned and back on her head. "I can do that myself," she said. "Cleaning them is a little harder, but you have to let me do the things I can." "What're you getting so angry for?" he said. "You mad because I'm leaving you alone so long?" "No, I'm glad you're seeing Leonard; I was just saying." "Anything else you need before I go?" "Maybe a pillow behind my back." "Maybe or definitely?" "Yes, pillow. And if you could straighten out my feet. They're turned in and will stay that way unless you fix them." He straightened her feet on the foot rests, adjusted a bed pillow behind her till she said it felt right."Anything else?" "Nope. Oh, maybe one or two of the almond macaroon cookies," and he said "One or two? Don't force me to make all the decisions for you." "Okay, then three in case you're late getting back and I get very hungry." "If you do, you can wheel yourself to the refrigerator, no?" "Sometimes it's not so easy. The doorways are so narrow here, even with the special hinges, and the new chair's an inch wider than the old one." "So let's only bring in the old chair from now on if it's just for a day." "It's not as comfortable. And the trip in and back? I don't know how I stood it all these years. 'Stood it.' Listen to me." "I let you stand it because Blue Cross only pays for a new one every five years. I shouldn't have been so cheap. Next time we'll bring in both chairs and you'll use the old one when it's easier to." "You don't want to be dragging in both, and it's really not a problem. Just a bit more difficult with the doorways and rolling over the thresholds without, getting stuck." "Then let's get rid of the apartment. Seriously, it costs so much and we hardly use it," and she said "But I love this place. And where would we stay? Not in a hotel when we come in for a week or two. And I couldn't get into my father's tiny bathrooms and I wouldn't use a portable potty outside one. I wouldn't even bring it to his apartment. Forget the idea. Also, what I can use before you go is a kukicha tea in your travel mug so it stays warm." "Jesus, why didn't you say so before? It takes time to prepare and I got to get out of here." "Then go. I'll make it." "You won't be able to pour or carry it without burning yourself. And if you do burn yourself at the stove, let's say, and the phone drops out of your lap because you brought it with you and slides out of reach of your reacher or you can't use the phone because of your scalded hands, what would you do? I'd call and you wouldn't answer and I'd get so worried I'd drive right back. I'll make the tea. And I'm sorry for those last remarks. You no doubt could manage things, just not hot tea." He went into the kitchen. "While you're in there—" she said. "But I already told you about the macaroons. Oh God, what's happening to my mind? I forget so much and so quickly. It's supposed to be symptomatic of either my disease or the medicine I take for it; I forget. That last line would be a good example that my mind's still sharp if I'd said it as a joke intentionally." "What's that you're saying?" though he'd heard it. "Wait'll I come in. I'm busy, and sound doesn't travel well into the back part of the kitchen." He made tea and brought it and the macaroons in.

Before that, after her morning stint on the potty and after he got her back on the bed and had catheterized and exercised her, he stroked her thighs and she said "What are you doing?" and he said "You know," and got on his knees beside the bed and kissed her shoulder and slid his hand under her shirt and bra and said "Do you mind?" and she said "No, although I have to admit I'm still feeling pissy to you because of what you said last night," and he said "When?" and she said "When you were getting me ready for sleep," and he said "What did I say? I forget," and she said "Typical, and convenient," and he said "You know me; I say stupid things I don't mean. Whatever it was, I'm sorry," and she said "Want me to tell you what it was?" and he said "Not now," and kissed her and while they were kissing some more he put his hand inside her pad and began rubbing her and after she was making these sounds for a while he stood up and took off his clothes and raised her shirt and bra to her neck and pulled her pad off and got on the bed. It took him a while to get hard, he even had to feel it to see if it was, and then thought "Now's a good time, because once it's in there, it'll stay," and tried but got limp before he could get it in. "Maybe we need that lubricant," he said, and got some in the bathroom and dabbed it on his penis and pulled himself till he was hard and went back to the living room and got on top of her again but it went limp or didn't stay stiff enough to stuff in. "Let me," she said, and she did some things to him and he said "That should do it," and tried again. "Let's just give it up," he said. "You've been patient, done everything you could, but I doubt anything's going to work. I probably have too much on my mind distracting me, though I can't think what other than my apprehension at seeing Leonard after so long and the state he could be in and now my inability to do this with you," and sat up. "I'm sorry," and she said "Why? It happens. I'll take a raincheck," and he said "Because I got you started when you didn't really want to, and now I no longer want to myself. Actually, I do, but can't. Next time," and she said "Want to wait a few minutes?" and he said "No, as I said, my mind, things on it, and that I have to get out of here. I told Tessie I'd be there around noon. She might not go today but if she does she'll meet me there, to make my first time easier, so I don't want to be late. And the radio. Who the hell can make love with a news show on, and such boring stuff too? Tornado specialists in Oklahoma, the dwindling salmon run in Maine. Who cares unless you live there?" and got up and shut it off. "I should have thought of that earlier. It might have helped. And my glasses? Jesus, I've never made love with them on. That might have had something to do with it also, though I don't see how if I didn't know they were there," and took them off. "No, I need them if I'm going to find my things and get out of here," and put them on and looked at her, thinking she'd find the whole thing comical. Her arms were out to him and she said "My sweetie, take the glasses off, remember where you put them, and keep the radio off and come back to bed, if just for a quickie. Doesn't work, no big deal, but we'll have fun trying," and he said "I don't want to risk fizzling out again. I'll take a raincheck too. Or we'll turn them in at the same time." She said "As far as the risk of fizzle goes, I don't think you should worry. Even if it does seem to happen a little more frequently for both of us than a few years ago, that shouldn't be surprising. Age, three thousand or so hits, my illness, the limitation of positions because of it. Don't be concerned, because it certainly doesn't bother me." "Okay," he said, "let's give it another whirl. All this talk about it and seeing you there has got me going, and so what if it ends up a bust. Although I don't understand why it did today. I started it, felt great doing it, then plop. Maybe something to do with food and what I drank last night. Chinese, and two martinis for me in addition to a carafe of that terrible jug wine the restaurant gave for free—the alcohol alone could have done it. And even though they say they don't, maybe they put something like MSG in the food to enhance the taste buds but which also might reduce the libido." "Didn't seem to to me," she said, "and I ate almost as much as you," and he said "Only the male then, and it reduces the female's taste buds. And possibly the aspirins I took before bed to offset the inevitable bad effects of the alcohol this morning had something to do with it. I was also a little on edge the phone would ring and we wouldn't know what to do, ignore or answer it, but either choice, or just lying there thinking what to do, breaking up our concentration on sex," and dialed their number so the phone would give a busy signal to anyone calling. He got back on the bed, they kissed and fondled and he eventually got hard and wanted to put it in but thought let the excitement build a few more minutes, and continued kissing and rubbing her and then got on top and tried sticking it in but went limp. "That should do it," he said, getting off her. "We tried, did our best, or what we could under the pressure of knowing I had to be out of here soon, and it didn't work. It's sort of like writing a short story. You sit down at the typewriter and punch out three to four first drafts of different stories you don't like and know you'll never go back to, but at least you put in an honest writing day. But the next day you write the first draft of a story you like and know you'll spend the next two weeks to a month on—the time part of this analogy has to be worked on, as I suppose a lot else—and which may even, as it's happened a number of times, turn into a novel. Or else the next day you also write several first drafts of stories you don't like, though again you made a strong effort but are now beginning to worry nothing good is coming and that you may be creatively drained for the time being. But the day after that—it's never taken longer than three writing days —the first draft of a story you'll want to spend weeks to a month on will come and usually on the first try."

Before that, after he'd made her breakfast and given it to her in the living room, he said "I'm going to call home. Jackie should be up now, right?" and she said "If she isn't, the answering machine will pick up and she'll call us," and he dialed and Jackie answered and he said "So how's it going, my darling?" and she said "Fine," and he said "What you do last night?" and she said "I went to Marina's house," and he said "Sounds okay; how'd you get there?" and she said "Her dad drove me," and he said "What you do there?" and she said "Had pizza and watched a movie," and he said "So her father drove you home?" and she said "Sure, how else?" and he said "Marina come with you?" and she said "What are you saying?" and he said "Just that if she did, it was nice, because she might think you'd be uncomfortable driving alone with her dad," and she said "Why? He's a nice man. You worried about him?" and he said "Absolutely not. I've met him. Did he wait in the car till you got inside?" and she said "He came in, because I asked him, and checked all the rooms. I knew nobody could be in the house, but I was still a little afraid," and he said "We shouldn't leave you alone there even for a night unless you're having a friend sleep over," and she said "I'm all right. Just last night because of all the lightning and thunder and stuff," and he said "Oh yeah? Lightning and thunder? Nothing like that here and it's beautiful out now," and Loretta said "No. We had plenty early this morning," and he said "Did you hear that? I must've slept through it. —How'd you know it was early morning?" he said to Loretta and she said "I looked at my watch." "She sleeps with her watch on. So I guess the storm came up from the south. What time you get home?" and she said "Don't be mad. Around one. But I got enough sleep today and Marina's father didn't mind driving me home so late," and he said "I'm not mad. One o'clock's pushing it, but it is a weekend. We won't be home till around eight," and she said "That late?" and he said "Maybe sooner. I'm going to see my friend Leonard in what's sort of like an asylum for people with Alzheimer's and other dementia. Actually, since I'll be there an hour and a half at the most and plan to get there at noon, we should be leaving here at three. Still, that means seven or so till we get back," and she said "Can you get some food for me at Zen Palate?" and he said "Oh, God, sure, I guess. I was going to go by way of George Washington instead of Lincoln Tunnel, since I think there's an Italian street festival downtown that'll stall traffic. But all right, though add another half hour to the time we get home, probably more, because I'll have to go to Broadway, find a spot, park, and so on." "That's okay. Can you write these down? Basil roll, spinach wonton soup, sesame medallions. That's all I want, and maybe some yam fries. You and Mommy like them too." "I think I can remember that, since you have the same things every time, but I've a menu here if I don't. So, everything all right? And I'm not going to ask you about schoolwork and the painting you said you had to hand in," and she said "I'm taking care of everything." "Good. I'll get Mommy. I love you, sweetheart," and she said "Bye, Dad," and he put Loretta on. He went into the kitchen for a carrot, thought "Why doesn't she ever say she loves me? I don't get it. Even when I feed her the obvious line, there's never an 'I love you' or even a 'me too' in return." When he got back to the living room he said "Oh, you off already?" and she said "She seemed talked out and eager to get to her art work, and I assumed you'd fill me in." "Did she say she loves you at the end?" and she said "Just as she probably did to you." "She never says it to me anymore. She also never lets me kiss her and of course doesn't volunteer a kiss or even hold out her cheek for one at what you'd think would be the appropriate time, like when she says goodnight. If I make the slightest move to kiss, she ducks her head or steps aside. I have to catch her to kiss her, and boy does she hate that. She even flinches when I touch her. A simple hand on her shoulder—instinctive or protective on my part—flinch.

She acts as if I once sexually abused her and she only recalled the memory two years ago, for that's when all this started happening. I've never done anything like that. I've always tried to be tactful, modest and decorous as I can around both kids. Our lovemaking—I'm the first to say keep it low. I haven't even walked around the house in undershorts in a long time, certainly not when I know one of them is there, and they're boxers and especially roomy, the least potentially offensive kind." "It's just a phase, and I wasn't aware. Maybe you should talk it over with her," and he said "I can't; she'd deny. She'd think I'm criticizing her. And then she'd be confused, thinking 'Now he's going to want me to kiss him and say I love him every time.' I'm old; maybe I'm ugly to her. The neck that's going, the sinking chin, and who knows what she imagines about my breath. But not even to let me pat her hand? I didn't want to hold it; I know that's been off limits for years. Really, it was as if I'd stuck it with a fork the way she drew it back. Gabrielle was never like that. She even tries to hold my hand sometimes when we walk, but I can't. If somebody saw it who didn't know she was my daughter, I'd feel peculiar. We should call her. We haven't spoken to her in days, and didn't she have the flu last time we talked to her?" and she said "That was weeks ago; she's fine." "Anyway," and he dialed Gabrielle's number. She said "Hi, Daddy," and told him, when he asked what she's been up to, about the painting she's very excited about she's been doing in her figure class.

And her roommate. "She continues to spray air freshener in our room and is always surprised I don't like the smell and her spraying noxious chemicals in my face and that we never used them at home. I don't know what to do." "Say you get sick from it and it makes you want to throw up. Then go to the bathroom and make retching noises and flush the toilet a lot and tell her that next time you might not be able to catch it in time. How else can I help you? We're on a roll," and she said she's having trouble coming up with a good theme for a Faulkner paper she has to do on two of his novels they've read, and gave the titles. "Oh, those two; they're tough. Your mother would be much more help than I. I remember she read them straight through and knew what was going on and the biblical connections, and none of the language seemed to stop her. Me, call me what you will—blockhead and dunce would be good for starters—but I couldn't get through most of his novels except the two or three easiest," and she said "I love them, *Absalom, Absalom*, the most, and had no trouble understanding them…excuse me," and he said "No need to. As a writer I should be a better reader, but I admit I'm an idiot. What else is new with you?" and she mentioned a movie she saw that she liked, the Nietzsche/Freud course she's now glad she's taking, the weather. "And there?" and he said "There's fine. You know, we're in New York. I'm driving up today to see my friend Leonard in a hospital for the mentally…well, it's like Alzheimer's, he has," and she said "What a shame. Such a nice man," and he said "Yes, a nice man, now becoming a nice vegetable. No, that was wrong, and according to his wife it's made him not so nice, but maybe he'll miraculously escape." "From the hospital?" and he said "I meant his illness, through some medication or operation. But think of it. No, don't. Young kids, nice wife, home he owns, job he likes, and he loved writing; like me, I don't think he ever had a block. But his wife thinks he's going to be stuck in that joint or one comparably miserable for the rest of his life. A horrifying thought and I've only touched the top of it. But I should drop it. So depressing, only I should have them. Tell me, anything else doing with you?" "Not really, and you?" "You know me. Never much to say on the phone. Maybe never anywhere, which is actually something Leonard would say of himself and I've stolen it. Always putting himself down. But artfully and comically, except when he was talking about fiction. Then he had opinions. He could have helped you with your paper. So, having nothing to say, I'm going to say toodle-de-do and put Mommy on, and it's been wonderful talking to you," and she said "Goodbye, Daddy, I love you," and he said "Love you too. That reminds me. Mommy told me to ask you this. Would you know, because we haven't a clue, any reason why Jackie jerks away from me whenever I so much as touch her hand or try, God forbid, to kiss her on the cheek goodbye or goodnight? Okay, the cheek business I can see. Doesn't want to be kissed by my sloppy lips. But looking hostilely and even disgustedly at me when I just barely graze her hand?" and she said "I've never seen her do that." "Yup. For two years now; I've been counting. Maybe you could ask her why. Nah, too devious, getting someone to do my prying, and I wouldn't want you to snitch, and of course you wouldn't. But you sure she's never said anything? Spoke about what a shit I am? Imagined I did something to her? But if she had told you in confidence, or what looked like it, it's good you're not telling me it. Loyalty to your sister; it's important," and she said "I'm not telling you because she never said anything. But yes, if she wanted me to keep something a secret, I would," and he said "Good, that's good. Sorry for bringing it up. Bye-bye, my darling," and she said "Bye, Daddy, I love you," and he said "Same here to you," and gave the phone to Loretta. "You liar," she said to him when she got off the phone, and he said "Why, what I do?" and she said "Are you kidding? Now if I told you what you said you'd just compound the compounded lie, so I won't even answer you. Waste of words." "Okay, okay, don't get sore at me. I thought if I had your support when I asked her—my requests alone usually don't amount to much—there'd be a better chance she'd divulge it. Credit me, at least, for being earnest in wanting to find out. But nothing to divulge, I suppose. And that's, I swear, the truth." She shut her eyes and nodded. What's that mean? he thought. Best not to ask.

Before that, he looked at his watch, thought Getting late; she'll be mad if he doesn't wake her, and raised the shades and said "Rise and shine, my dear. It's ten to nine. I've got to get out of here by eleven-thirty at the latest and it takes you two hours to get ready." "Give me five more. Till nine." He didn't mind. He'd finish his coffee and read some more of the paper and stretch it out to fifteen. Should he lower the shades? Not for such a short time. A huge tanker was moving north. River's so wide, he thought, now looking at it from his typing table in the kitchen, but looks much narrower when one of these monster ships is on it. It'd be nice to be alone on a little boat in the middle of the river, maybe sail across it to Jersey for a coffee at one of the public docks there. But what do you do when a big tanker approaches? Scratch the idea, and he usually gets seasick on boats anyway. Except the QE2. Best rest he's ever had, and England to New York on standby, so a relatively cheap trip too. Loretta well then and five months pregnant with Jackie. Gabrielle looked after by English nannies all day in the ship's nursery, so nothing to do but read, eat, swim, jog around the ship and see movies, and make love whenever they wanted to. Finished his coffee and the paper, toasted a quarter slice of bagel till it was crisp and ate it with nothing on it, and then thought "My goodness; it's ten after," and went into the living room and said "Gotta get up. I gave you twelve minutes instead of ten, I'm sorry," turning the clock on top of the TV so it didn't face her. "Great day out," pulling off her unbleached cotton blanket and folding it. "Ideal temperature and low humidity expected," tugging the bed pillow out from between her knees. "Nothing much in the news. No wars, ethnic rows, suicide bombings, retaliatory strikes, ghastly murders or accidents or plane crashes. The world was seemingly at peace the day before yesterday—I'm only now reading Saturday's paper; Sunday's will be waiting for us at home—and nobody of significance died. In fact the number of paid obits in the *Times* was exceptionally small, and a review of a book about bankers and banking, or maybe it was bakers and baking—I only gave it a quick look and my glasses were dirty then. Plus a slew of dance reviews. Ever read one? This movement and smashing set, that taped score and flat foot, etcetera. Deadly dull," and took off her soft boots and put them and the blanket into the small valise on the cocktail table. "And you're missing the most enormous tanker on the river. You're also not talking or opening your eyes; how come? Oh well. It's so long and going so slow that after ten minutes the front of it's still parallel to our building. What do you call the front again?" and she said "Bow." "Bow, right; aft is back and eyes are open," and she said "Aft is toward the stern, which is the rear. My first husband, he owned a boat and taught me the terms. We once sailed from Massachusetts to North coastal Maine. I was new at it but not by the time it was over. He let me steer and eventually chart half the cruise," and he said "I remember you telling me, and what I missed out on. You as a relative youth, when your hair was almost bright blond. You as a mature woman with only a trace of blond anymore, or in your early thirties when I met you, isn't and wasn't bad either. But there's something about being young and tip-top healthy and vigorous and in love and the same age as your girlfriend or wife and both of you tasting from salt on a sailboat and tacking up, if that's what it's called, Downeast, if that's what it is." "It was lots of work and of course exhilarating, but took half the summer. I wouldn't call it sexy, though, if that part's bothering you. We were too tired," and he said "All the time, I'm hoping. It's the image I'd prefer, both of you not even trying," and she said "Not all the time, of course. We were in our twenties and both of us enjoyed sex. But that cramped bunk below was extremely uncomfortable." "Too cramped for making extensive love in a variety of positions," and she said "No, but I was always afraid I'd fall out of it, even when we were anchored. Once we made love, we slept in separate bunks. But the cruise almost drove us apart for good. Our exhaustion made us irritable, the sun made us sore, and also the boredom when there was no wind for an entire day. You had the choice of staying above and baking or going below and boiling, and we brought the wrong books." "What were they?" and she said "Thackeray, Tolstoi, Trollope. Harry's idea, and that we take turns reading to each other. We also thought we could write lots of poetry, but we only came out with one short poem each: both on fog." "So how'd you get the boat back to wherever he kept it—just turned around and sailed?" and she said "Why, what's that got to do with it?" and he said "You know me: keen on technical details; how you get from one room to the next, and how things turn out." "I stayed with friends in Maine and he sailed alone to Ipswich, where he stored the boat till the next year. Said he wanted time to think about us. We never took another long cruise together. Didn't think our marriage would hold up if we did." "I wish you two had split apart that first cruise. I might have met you on the rebound in Fairway, maybe the day after you got back. We both lived on the West Side then. And I would have said to you in the cheese department—a logical place for us since we both love cheese and it was when I was still allowed to eat it—having been immediately attracted to your sun- and sea-bleached hair and braised face when I spotted you in the wurst section, 'Excuse me, but would you know what a Gorgonzola de fongu is?' You would have thought me pitiful that I had to use such a stupid line to approach you, but ultimately...oh, what am I doing? I wish I had learned how to sail and was born with better sea legs. Then you and I could have gone out in a rented boat, maybe even for a two-day cruise. Twenty summers in Maine wasted on me, in that I hate blueberries, lobsters and sailing." He looked out the window. "Tanker just now finished passing." "Liar," she said, and he said "But you get the idea how long it is without seeing it, right?" He started to unbutton her pad. "Leave it on today. It's not that wet," and he said, feeling it—it was almost dry—"It's soaked. You could get a rash. That could end up being dangerous. Come on," and took it off, felt the mat underneath, it was dry, and said "Wet too," and pulled it out, put a towel under her, dropped the pad into the bathroom waste basket, turned the bathtub faucet on so she'd think he was rinsing the mat, which is what he does in the apartment when it's actually wet and then wrings it out, and hung it on the shower stall. Don't forget to pack it before you leave for home, he thought, and also to put all the trash out by the service elevator. He went back to the living room, said "Everything all right?" and she said "Yes, but you're taking so much time. I'm going to have to use the potty soon and I'm not protected." "Let me know if you have to go; I'll get you on it fast," and started the first set of exercises of the day. Stretching her leg and bending it back, he looked at her vagina slightly parted, though made sure she wasn't observing him—her eyes were shut. He liked looking at her down there when he exercised her. Peculiar? Not too. It's like having the radio on while he does it: helps pass the time, and also works him up. She probably knew he snuck looks and that was why he was always so eager to have her pad off when he exercised her, but didn't say anything, even this morning, figuring if it helped him do the chore, it was worth it.

Before that, he showered and stared at the bathroom mirror while he shaved and thought "Look at that puss. You're getting old, man, old? What're you talking about? You are old. You can always make yourself look younger in the mirror by turning this way and that, catching the light right and furrowing your brow and so on, but who would you be fooling? Me, man, me. I don't look so old. I'm not bald, gray, lined, beginning to shrivel. Truly, though, face it: the chin, neck, especially the eyes. Rhino eyes, they look like, the bags and sagging lids. Your dad's eyes when he was your age and maybe even older. Ah, what's it get you, thinking of it? So long as you can still lift weights and run a mile or two without panting and do your writing and essential thinking and get a hard-on most times when you want to and keep it, you're okay."

Before that, he needed to quickly satisfy his hunger. He got the jar of hulled sunflower seeds out of a kitchen cabinet and was about to take a swig of them when he dropped it. Didn't know how it happened. Maybe his palm was sweaty from his run, because the jar just seemed to slip out of his hand. The cap came off, jar rolled and most of the seeds spilled out. "Damn," he said, "why does everything have to fall?" He swept the seeds together and tried getting them all on the dustpan, but there were too many; the ones he didn't get he'd do in a second sweep. His hand shook when he was carrying the pan to the garbage can under the sink, maybe because he was concentrating too hard on keeping it straight, and half the seeds fell off. "Shit!" he said, emptying the pan into the can, and Loretta said from bed "What's wrong? Hurt yourself?" "No, just a dumb blunder. Go back to sleep. It's still early." Ought to be an expression, he thought: "Trying to get too much on a dustpan." It's good, he should write it down, but what for? At the moment he thought of it, if Loretta had been fully awake, he might have repeated it to her. But expressions are coined every day and coining them's not what he wants to be known for.

Before that, he sat on the stairs in the outside hallway and put his sneakers on. Didn't want to chance waking Loretta by putting them on inside. She might want to get up, and he wanted to get his run, shower and shave out of the way before he took care of her. Ran down the six flights of stairs. It was a great feeling, always was, holding onto the banister and running and leaping round and round the stairs till he reached the bottom, and opened the door slowly because someone in the lobby might be standing in front of it. The doorman was sitting in one of the chairs, and Irv said hello. "Welcome back," Emilio said, getting up and shaking his hand. "How's Loretta?" and he said "Fine as can be expected, thanks. And your family?" and Emilio said "Also good. Kids with you?" and he said "Nah, one's away in college and younger one never wants to leave her hamster and friends. And the building? No major setbacks?" and Emilio said "Nothing since you were last here, I think, unless you didn't hear about Ivy in 9J more than a month ago. Killed herself. Wasn't sick or anything, they said, just depressed. Did it from a book. Lots of pills and vodka, put a bag over her head and candles all around her, but they were out by the time she was found two days later. The smell. Fortunately, I wasn't on duty. Dionis was and he says he still gets nightmares of it. And the candles. She could've burnt down the building, because she didn't even put them on metal trays—just the wood floor. Poor lady." "I don't recall her. Young, old?" and Emilio said "On your line, J, two above you. Very skinny. They said she didn't eat and always threw up. She had a little white dog, Freddy." "I know who you mean. Very polite, very nice. Every time I saw her she was walking the dog. What happened to it? Wouldn't it have barked?" "She got rid of it a week before. She loved it. Held it more than she walked it. But all she said was, when I asked where's Freddy, 'With my brother in the country for a week.' She had no brother, they found out. No family, and she's been out of a job for months, and nobody knows where Freddy went. I would've taken him if she wanted to give him away, but I didn't know to ask. Freddy and I got along, and what a beauty; could be a show dog, she said, if she wanted him to." "So what did they do with the apartment?" and Emilio said "It's being fixed up now, and they'll get three times what she paid." "What happens to her possessions when there are no immediate survivors?" and Emilio said "It's stored, they make notices in newspapers, and nobody claims it, the landlord gets it or calls a charity. Some rich stuff too. Mirrors, rugs; her mother's." "Who pays for the storage, the city?" and Emilio said "I don't know; it never came up." "And if she had bank savings and such, I wonder where that goes, but what's the difference. It's awful, I'm so sorry. I suppose she left no note." "Nothing they found, or a will." "But everything else in the building's okay?" and Emilio said "The usual tenant complaints and plumbing problems. It's an old building. Did you see your bathroom wall?" and he said "No, why? Don't tell me another leak." "From 8J. They had to open your wall to get to the pipes. I guess they did a good job in plastering and repainting." "And cleaning up, because I didn't notice a thing." "They didn't know where to reach you, so they just went in. Don't let them know I told you, but you should be more careful. I know you don't live here most of the time, and I keep my mouth shut. But somebody else who works here—you know, for money—or a tenant in back who wants a river view, can tell the landlord. Because your rent's so low, they can want you evicted. Law says it has to be your main residence at least fifty-one percent of the year. That's what I learned when they got rid of 15K. In three months, though she spent a fortune fighting it, she was on the street. This is New York. You know, you were born here; money rules this city. Because of your wife, she's so sweet and her illness and she's had the apartment before even you came, maybe they let you stay till the end of your lease." "Whew, this is really something you're telling me. But I don't know what we can do about it. I suppose just hope nobody squeals. Anyway, got to get my run in before Loretta wakes up." "Give her my regards. I won't see her because I'm off in ten minutes," and he said "Will do, and thanks for the tip," and patted Emilio's shoulder and went through the revolving door. Damn, shit, piss, he thought, waiting for the cars to pass before he could run across the street to the park. So now he's got the apartment to worry about. He's sure the landlord knows and that Emilio probably told him and that the eviction notice will be coming soon. Fight it? What case do they have and who's got the money for lawyers? He won't tell Loretta about it today. She'll get too upset, and maybe it won't happen for months. Mile down to 97th Street inside the park, then back up along the park side of Riverside Drive, and at 116th went up the hill to the Chinese restaurant on Broadway to get a take-out menu off the window. Before they leave he'll order some food for tonight, things Jackie and Loretta will especially like. "Poor lady" is right, he thought, as he walked back to the building. Saw her a hundred times and never knew her name or what apartment she was in. Nice smile and pretty face and always a pleasant hello, but such a pitifully thin body. Never saw her with another person, though she talked a lot to the doormen when she was downstairs. Doesn't think he'll tell Loretta about this either just yet, since Ivy died too much like Loretta's mother—from a book but without the candles. He doesn't want to say this is a sad world, but it is. "Say, nice to see you," Dionis said when Irv got back to the building, and he pressed the elevator button for him. "Staying a little longer this time?" and he said "Afraid not. Just came in to see my wife's father and a very sick friend of mine. But we'll be in soon for a while. How you doing?" and Dionis said "I had some problems, thanks, and had to take a few days off, but I'll be all right. Nothing physical this time or I can't get rid of by just not thinking of it."

"Well, that's a good simple cure if it's effective," and Dionis said "You didn't hear?" and he said "9J? Ivy? Terrible, awful," and Dionis said "Of all people, with all the things I've been going through with my ulcers and back, I had to be the one to find her, with the handyman. But he's used to it, he said, from his other building before here, which was huge and had lots of old-timers." Elevator door opened and Irv said "I'd like to talk more but left my wife in sort of a precarious position and don't want her to fall." "Of course; last thing you need," and pressed his floor button and Irv got in. They stood looking at each other a few seconds; the elevator, only from the lobby, had a mind of its own, the tenants liked to say. "Everything else in the building all right? I mean, I know about the J-line flood. Oops," when the door started to close, "we'll continue this next time," but Dionis held it open with his hand and said "Excuse me, my apologies, I forgot to ask about your wife. Sometimes I think I have all the problems," and he said "We're fine, thanks; things are looking good for all of us,' and Dionis said "Glad to hear that; such a brave lovely lady. Please give her my best," and let the door close.

Before that, he awoke, thought it was still early. Not even light out, or maybe it was just cloudy. Got his watch off the side table by the bed and pressed the button that made the watch face light up. Twenty to seven, so it must be cloudy. He should get up, he thought. It'll give him time for coffee and reading and exercising in the kitchen with the door shut, going

for a run and then maybe to the market on 110th to buy some
food for home and bagels for Jackie at the bagel shop next
door. And he has to turn Loretta over on her back. Can't forget
that, though lots of mornings he'd like to. Did it every day
around four-thirty, or tried to around that time, so was two
hours behind. He already made her angry enough last night. If
she asks what time it is, he'll say "Little before six." She
sleeps with her watch on, but hers doesn't have a light. Usually
he woke around four-thirty, checked his watch, hoping it was
much earlier so he could sleep more, and after he peed, drank
some water and turned her over and got her comfortable, went
back to bed for another two hours. Here he slept against the
wall, so he edged himself off the foot of the bed, pushing a
table with the TV on it so he could get out. His chest ached
from the stretching he did with a stretch band last night. His
body had been stiff from the drive in, so he felt he needed to
limber up. He peed, drank a glass of water and went back to
the living room. She was on her side facing out, same position
he put her in when she went to sleep. He pulled the blanket
off her, a bit too roughly, he thought. It could seem he was
angry at her, which he wasn't. Should have first said, which he
usually did, "Loretta, you up? I'm getting you on your back."
He got the towels out that had been wedged in behind her to
keep her on her side. He had to tug at the pillow between her
legs to get it out. Way the knees had clamped it you'd almost
think, he thought, her legs were strong enough to stand on and

walk. One of the soft boots had come off and he put it back on. If he didn't, she's ask him to. He stuck his arm under her knees and lifted her onto her back. Her pad in front looked like a white bikini bottom and was kind of sexy. He stretched out her legs and put a pillow under her feet, then spread the blanket over her. "All right?" and she said "Something under my right knee, please?" and he put a couch pillow there and she said "Thank you." He exercised in the kitchen and thought This is going to be quite a day. Getting her up and all the things that go with that. Then if she still wants to shampoo, which she said last night she did—it'd been days and she forgot to before she left—helping her with that too. Then getting her set up for the time he'd be away. Seeing Leonard. Just finding the place might be a problem. He's not good on roads he hasn't been on and highway connections he hasn't made. Later getting Loretta set for the drive back. Packing, and loading the car, though that shouldn't be much, and the long drive home. But once there, what a relief. Get Loretta inside the house first, on the john, her medicine, snack, tea, then the things out of the van and put away. Again, not that much. Probably a wash started for the clothes and stuff she used in New York and the trip there and back. Prepare dinner and sit in his easy chair while some of the food's cooking and have a vodka and grapefruit juice, and read his mail if there's any and part of today's *Times* and *Sun*. Nah, won't have time. And he'll have to get Loretta back in the wheelchair. He'll have his drink while preparing dinner and the radio on to some good music. Or no music, he'll have had enough of it in the car. Just quiet, the natural sounds of the house and outside, and talking to Jackie: "So how are things? What'd you do? Anyone call while we were gone?" Then they'll have dinner. With a good wine. "Good" meaning anything that cost him more than eight bucks. Maybe, to save time, since Loretta and Jackie eat different things for dinner anyway—he usually just has a salad and wine and sometimes a slice of bread (has to remember to pick up a bread here plus another to freeze and a chocolate croissant for Jackie tomorrow morning and of course several plain bagels for her)—he should call her and say they'll be home after her normal dinner time, so she should make something for herself before. There's gnocchi and tortellini in the freezer, but have what you want. If she says, as she's done, can she send out for pizza, he'll say, as he always does, he doesn't like those pizza guys delivering to the house when she's alone. Also, he'll say, keep the doors locked when she's home and turn the carport lights on when it starts to get dark and switch on some lights in different rooms.

Before that, he dreamed. Loretta in one woke up and said she had a dream she was pregnant and told him and he didn't seem surprised. "That gives me an idea," he said, slipping off his bathrobe. He glanced down, thinking he had an erection sticking straight out and she was looking at it. "Uh-oh," he said, when he saw he had a carrot for a penis, "no can do. Darn.

All my life I've loved carrots. The raw kind have been my favorite food for fifty years. But I hate them with a passion now." In another dream he was at the top of a snowy hill in Riverside Park with Gabrielle, who looked around five. He set her new toboggan on the ground and pointed it down the hill. "Watch me, Daddy," she said, sitting on it, and he said "Not so fast, kiddo. I have to explain how to use it first. You grab the handrails and hold on. You steer by shifting your weight this way and that. If it looks like you're going to crash into something and no other sled's right behind you, jump off. We'll go down a few times together till you get the hang of it," and she said "Fiddle food," and started down the hill. "Wait," he said. Oh my goodness, he thought, I pointed it down the wrong side of the hill. The other side's for sledding. This one has a highway cutting across it at the bottom. No wonder we're the only ones on it and all the noise of people having fun is behind us. "Jump off," he yelled at her, "or you'll get killed." She kept going. Cars were whizzing past both ways on the highway. "What am I going to do?" he screamed. "Oh God, help me." He held his arm out to her. It started to grow and kept growing till it was above her. He snatched her off the sled seconds before it reached the highway and was smashed by a car and brought her back to the top of the hill. "That was close," Jackie said. "Where'd you come from?" he said. "I thought you were with Mommy. And you just spoke your first words. What are you, two? Your sister's first was 'bird,' a single word, but yours was plural. Do you know what a plural is?" and she said "One, I'm one." "I've got to remember this. It's something I started doing with your sister and also your mother's first words after your births. I'll write them; my memory's lousy." He found a pen in his jacket pocket but nothing to write on. He wrote on his wrist: "They were close." Oh, go even further, he thought, and put the pen to his wrist again but couldn't remember her second sentence. In another he was carrying a long thin branch with a phone number on it and flowers coming out of the end, and said "Maybe I should send it to my mother in Florida rather than carrying it down." "Is she all right?" his former neighbor up the hill said, and he said "No, she has more than enough flowers around her, and what would she do with your old phone number? I should call her and ask. Excuse me," and he picked up a phone. "Oh gee, she never gave me her number and I don't even know where she is down there." In another he stood at a podium in front of a black-tie audience in the main ballroom of the Plaza and said into the microphone "Thank you. At the bottom of my heart I deeply appreciate this honor. 'Appreciate deeply'? I don't know if I'll be able to wear it well or do myself justice, but I accept without reservations. Though you should know it wasn't I who won it. 'Weren't I'? It was my wife and children and friends and all of you in the darkness out there. 'Were my wife and children'? I'm sorry, I'm so good at this that it's getting embarrassing, not that I should stop," and he stepped back from the podium. There was a smattering of applause. Then someone in the audience shouted out "Maestro, your speech was on fire. Get a hose and put it out and then hose down everything else you ever put down." The applause was louder now and there were some cheers and whistles. He stepped back to the microphone and said "I should go home," and looked for Loretta at their table but she wasn't there. Nor were the three couples who had been at the table with them. In another dream he said to his graduate class "I'm pleased as Punch to have my old pal Lenny Fisk as your guest critic today and also to talk about his own writing and anything else he might have in mind. Let me say straight off that I've read all his published work, which is considerable, and have admired it as much as I have any writer's the last thirty years." "We once read together," Leonard said, "you remember that?" "Sure. With another writer. He read a story about a Cuban baseball player. Sort of a Garcia Marquez–like fantasy of a guy who wants to escape Castro's Cuba to play in the big leagues in America and he hit a homer out of a Havana ballpark and flies with it all the way to Wrigley Field in Chicago. Boy, did that story stink, and the writing couldn't have been worse." "I wrote that story," Leonard said, "and read it that day too." "I know; I was just testing you. You're fine. You're sharp. You're in great shape all around. Look at him," he said to the class. "He looks ten years younger than I when he's actually three years older to the day. And he has the energy of a kid and the mental quickness of I don't know what, so why would anyone think something's wrong with his memory and health?" "Please, you made a real dumb mistake," Leonard said. "Or as we used to say in Bensonhurst, an 'oh my faux pas.' Admit it: you never liked my work and have been an insincere flatterer because you knew I could continue to help you find a book publisher and get your stories into good literary magazines." "Not true. You barely lifted a finger to get yourself published. That was honorable, one could say, scribbling just for the love of it, but impractical if you wanted to reap the side benefits of publication, like a teaching position and writing fellowships and awards. I was the one who got you your two book publishers, who happened to be mine at the time. I even wrote a blurb for your first book, something I hated doing for anyone: they're so goddamn dishonest and self-promoting. 'A sterling debut. Fisk is a cross between late Chekhov and early Hemingway, with a smidgen of Babel and the Singer brothers thrown in.' I was the one who told you about new magazines to send to, soon as I heard of them, while you never told me of any till you'd been rejected by them several times. I got you your first adjunct teaching jobs. Without them you never would have been offered that tenure-track position later on. The Cuban missile business was only to prove to myself you were in good mental condition, and I knew I'd really have to use my imagination to do it or you'd catch on and fake being crazy just to have fun with me. I have liked lots of your work, and some of it very much. The humor, timeliness, simple language, lucid style, great dialogue and lively characters and situations. The get-to-the-point and don't-beat-around-the-bush-or-a-horse-after-it's-dead and tell-the-damn-story-already and get-out-once-you've-made-your-point but tie-it-up-tidily-with-no-loose-knots and a-pox-on-all-literary-and-mostly-stolen-modernistic-tricks of it. And that you never let anything get in the way of your writing, never take a day off from it unless you've a crippling flu, for instance, or scads of breadwinning schoolwork to do." Leonard stared at him through all this, saying "Yeah, yeah, yeah, yeah," and when Irv finished, put his dirty handkerchief to his nose, said "Excuse me," and pretended to sneeze, but instead of an "ah-choo" he shouted "Horseshit." "Okay," Irv said, "we're not going to get anything out of anything today, so class dismissed," and one of the students said "Hey, Professor Hotshot, I paid big bucks to get into this program. So I'm in hock up to my gwazuzzi and want my money's worth, like my story workshopped as it was supposed to be, with or without your friend." "Kid's got a point, Len. As a teacher yourself, what would you do if you were me in this situation?" and Leonard said "What you should have done years ago: give up, pack a few books and leave your typewriter, gather your family and drive back to New York and drop me off at my door, because I can't take this place." "I'd love to—just to have all that freedom and time to do what I truly want to—but my kids have to go to school and then college and the cats like the outdoors. As for my type-writer, I can't; even if you were being untypically sarcastic to me, it's the only thing you or I use." In another, the last before he woke up, he and Loretta were standing on a small airstrip beside a single-prop plane, its propellor spinning as if it were about to take off. "Get in, make yourself comfortable," the pilot said, and Irv said "Wait, where the heck you think we're going? I made no plane reservations, nor do we have tickets, and we left our passports home," and the pilot said "It's your private flight, sir, booked and paid for long in advance. You want to get from one tropical island to another around here, this is the only way to do it." "You don't recall, dear?" Loretta said. "You're on paid leave for a year and we're off on a much needed vacation." "Can't be; I would have known and been giddy. I don't go to work tomorrow I'll be fired, and then what'll we do for money? If the flight were free I still wouldn't take it. Bad weather's predicted and these planes are patently unsafe. More accidents happen with them than with washing machines." "Nonsense," the pilot said. "Even if it were like you say, once we got above cloud cover, it'd be sun all the way. Please, folks, climb aboard. Time's money and money's the times." Loretta and the kids got in the plane and took seats by the windows facing him. Loretta walked, he thought. This must be a vacation. "Come on, Daddy," Gabrielle said; "without you the plane doesn't fly." Well, he thought, dying with them is better than their dying without him, and maybe he is on leave and the plane's fine and weather will be great, and he climbed in and sat beside Loretta. It turned out to be a seaplane and it skipped along the water's surface before rising. "Smooth takeoff?" the pilot said. "Just watch the ascent. It'll be like floating in heaven." "Smooth," the kids said, "smooth," and then there were dark spiraling clouds all around, fierce lightning and thunder and slashing rain and the plane was shaking violently and started to nosedive. Oh God, will things never stop dropping? he thought. "I knew it," he said, "this is it," and the pilot said "Nonsense, we're nowhere near there yet. It's eighty-six miles to Socatumee, a mere fifty minutes flying time. Then, paradise, till you fly to the next paradise, each one more beautiful than the one before. I'm your pilot for the week," and Irv said "You must mean 'for the weak,'" and the pilot said "If you like me, for the month if you want." Everyone but the pilot gripped their seat arms and the kids were going "Whee-e-e" as if they were sledding down a hill, and then the plane pulled out of the dive and straightened out about ten feet above water and flew over it like that, waves splashing the windows. "We're too close," Irv shouted to the pilot. "Get it up, get it up. Damn," he said to Loretta, "why did we think of doing such a stupid thing as getting on a small plane with such an inexperienced pilot?" and she said "We'll get out of it. And if we don't—I don't know everything—we'll at least all be together till the end. Isn't that what you also thought before?" They continued to fly about ten feet above the waves, the kids and pilot singing "Smooth, smooth, we're doing the smooth," the clouds darker and more spirally and the storm much worse.

Before that, he awoke an hour after he'd fallen asleep. Loretta was snoring loudly. Did that wake him? he thought. Probably not and it was the dream he just had, something where one of the kids was in danger, in a car or on a wagon speeding out of control down a hill. He shut his eyes but her snores kept him from dozing off. He could nudge her, but she'd get mad and say something like "What's with you? You woke me again after I told you not to." So he lay on his back but couldn't get to sleep; her snores and now whistles and some kind of bubbling sound from her mouth. He shook her gently. She continued to make noises. He turned over and over, hoping the motion and bed-bouncing would wake her or stop the noises. He turned on the light by him. If she asked what he was doing, he'd say he has to jot down a line before he forgot it. She didn't stir. Jesus, she's in deep. He shook her shoulder harder. "What? Why're you waking me? Now I'll never fall asleep." "Yes you will; it's still night." "You were making these strange noises and I thought something was wrong with your breathing. You all right? Need a handkerchief to blow it out? I've got one here." "Oh, stop it. Don't be a bully in bed. I'm sorry I've kept you up, but I can't help what I do in my sleep. It disturbs you so much, sleep in the girls' room." "I just might. But I like lying in this bed, lumpy as it is, and, if I can, holding you, especially your breasts." "Don't give me that, and don't hold me, especially my breasts. It'll keep me up more. Maybe you can't sleep because of all you drank tonight, so take some aspirins." "Drink? What are you talking about? Okay, I'll shut up; I want you to go back to sleep." He turned off the light, faced the wall, covered his exposed ear with his pillow. Though she started making noises again, he soon drifted off.

Before that, when Loretta was in bed and he was getting her set for sleep, she said "Better put the clothes I wore today into the overnight so we don't forget them tomorrow," and he said "Please, I'm doing one thing, tell me what else I have to do, later." "I was just saying—" and he said "You're always just saying, or too damn often. I'm in the middle of getting you breakfast and you say could I put your socks on. I'm strapping your chair down in the van and you say could I help you take off your jacket. I'm on my knees, goddamnit, and you're asking me this before I finish. All right, you need these things done. Your body's warm, your feet are cold, and you can't do them yourself. But give me a few seconds between chores. It's also the way you say it that bugs me. You don't say 'Excuse me, but when you're through doing that, could you help me take off my jacket?' You just say it, and I have to jump." "That's not true. I don't want you to jump and I don't know why you're getting so exercised over it. When I asked about the clothes, I didn't mean you should do it this moment. And you want all the civilities thrown in, I'll do it. A dozen thank-yous and pleases with each request if it will stop you from snapping at me like this. I am thankful for all the help you've given; I never suggested otherwise. What I'm not thankful for are these ridiculous arguments you try to start with me. I was only saying before that I don't want to leave my things behind and if we could take precautions to see that I don't. Don't pack them if you don't want to, but at least put them on the overnight bag so you don't forget them." "I'll put them," he said, "I'll put them," and got her bra, socks and jumper off the couch and threw them at the overnight on the coffee table. "Wonderful. A very important point you made there, and appropriately dramatic." "I'm not making any points. The hell with points. The hell with everything, you understand what I'm saying?" and she said "Not really. Listen, better we don't say anything more to each other tonight. You're losing control and acting like a jackass," and he said "I'll say, that business about not talking. Who the hell wants to talk to you anyway?" and she said "Thank you; very nice." "I'm sorry; I didn't mean it that way," folding her jumper and putting it in the overnight with her bra and socks. "But I'm not good at apologizing. Even when I say the right words and mean them, it doesn't sound like I do, so let's drop it." "Whatever you say. You want to drop it, it's dropped. It's best we both let our mouths dry up." "Right," he said, "though I'm not sure. Oh, dry, not letting air in, so not speaking. Right. Best, yes." Resumed getting her ready for sleep, didn't say anything and tried not to look at her face. Clock on top of the television: it was getting late, he was tired, wanted to get in bed. Art work around the room: most given by her artist friends; painting willed to her by her favorite graduate school teacher; a huge print, an engagement gift from her first husband thirty years ago, of Chekhov facing down what looked like Soviet policemen. Made no sense, even if they were supposed to be tsarist policemen. "Ready?" She nodded, and he flipped her to her side so she now faced the outside of the bed, wedged a pillow between her knees, small couch pillow under her bottom knee, covered her and, before she could remind him, since he usually forgot this, put a handkerchief by her face. Then he washed up, undressed, put his shirt over the side table lamp shade so the light wouldn't disturb her, and got into bed. He always kissed her on the lips after he covered her or got into bed. Not doing it tonight, he thought, had to be on her mind too. Probably something like "Surely he's not going to try to kiss me. He does, I'll turn my face away. But he can't be that dense or influenced by drink not to know it's the last thing I want now—that and his touching me. I hate the bastard sometimes. And he is; he acted like a real bastard. I don't know how I get to feel good about him again after he says things like that. But I always do and he, obvious as it is that he detests me while he's saying it, seems to forget everything he said by the next day and gets back to feeling good about me too."

Before that, they took a bus to her father's place on West 84th. Hyman said, when she asked if he'd been in contact lately with any of his old friends, that whenever he calls one he finds they're dying or just got diagnosed for cancer or broke a hip or showing signs of Alzheimer's and they're frightened what's going to happen to them from it or it's just normal memory loss and confusion from old age and he has to repeat his name several times before they realize who's calling, "even if most of them I know since primary school in Poland or met soon after your mother and me came here in '47. Or they're extremely depressed themselves—much worse than me and for a lot longer and are on all sorts of powerful drugs—and want to die. A couple of them even asked what method your mother used so they can also do it that way. Can you imagine such imbeciles? Asking me for her suicide directions she left, not two years after she died? So I should talk to them anymore? For what, so they can remind me of your mother and what I went through that day? They were close friends once—thirty of them, forty. We all fell on each other because of what we lost, and became like family. But when you get as old as we are and with our problems, it doesn't seem so important anymore. Besides, I don't feel like seeing anyone but my real family. You two make me feel good and seeing your kids makes me feel even better. I have something for them, by the way, before you go. But everybody else it's getting to be a nuisance and pain just going over to their homes or getting them things like drinks and snacks when they come here." "Oh boy," Irv said, "you really give me something to look forward to. I'm getting up there in years too," and Hyman said "You? You're young yet. You got plenty of time to be miserable. What are you, getting near sixty?" and he said "Cusping sixty-five and a hundred-percent Social Security checks." "Don't forget you have to pay taxes on it while you're still working. Not all, but almost. But you look well. You're fine. You never had to go through anything like what me and Helenka did, so you'll live longer and healthier than us." "Nothing? I've gone through nothing? All right. I won't boast. So you don't like to see friends. But movies? You've got one of the biggest multiplexes in the city right up the block. I know it's mostly crap they show, but seen anything recently you could recommend?" and Hyman said "I never go. They're all made for people sixty to seventy years younger than me and with entirely other experiences. TV I watch, the news only, a few minutes in the morning and an hour before bed at night. So far nobody gets naked on it or curses without being beeped." "Then theater. Some of what they do is interesting. You live in one of the best cities in the world for it. You can take a cab," and Hyman said "And get caught in traffic for an hour and with no guarantee of ever finding one back? Besides, those shows are so expensive that I'd have to buy a balcony seat. And none of those old theaters have elevators, so I'd have to walk up. My feet; it's no good. One thing working against the other." "Then you don't go out much, period," Irv said, "except maybe to see the doctor about your feet." "I go out. I got to eat, don't I? Because what should I do, call up and have the food delivered? Just put me in a prison cell and lock the door, if that's how I'm supposed to live. Zabar's. They know me, get me a cab so I can take my bags home. Food there's as good as any restaurant in the city." "Good, you're doing something you like," Loretta said, and he said "Of course. I walk in and crowded as it always is they say hello and shove me up front in the line. I never have to take a ticket. I've been going there forty years. More. Before then I used to drop in some weekends when we were still in the Bronx." "So they not only appreciate you for your business," Irv said, "but respect and like you. That's great." Hyman smiled: "Listen, like another drink? The last one I made was a little weak, I think. I can't drink it myself because of all the antibiotics Ravitzski's put me on, but I could tell I didn't pour enough." "Papa, he's had two already and we'll probably have wine at dinner, if you still feel like going out. Otherwise, we can order Chinese food in." "Sure we're going out, if it's no hardship on either of you. Because what's to stop me? My feet aren't that bad, and how often do I get to see you two? So I'll walk a little slower. You don't want to drag behind with me, shoot ahead and I'll catch up. I know where the place is. And one small drink won't kill him. He's had a long drive in and then coming down here by bus, so he needs to relax. And what I have is a special vodka a client brought back from Russia for me. You wouldn't be able to find it even in the best liquor store, so I'm making him another," and he stood up with a bit of a struggle and Irv said "I'll take care of it," and he put his hand up and said "No; in your home, not mine," and shuffled to the kitchen. "Maybe you want it even stronger this time," he yelled from the kitchen. "I don't want you to think because I said the vodka's so special, I'm holding it back. Or maybe the same amount with an ice cube and less V-8 juice in it," and Irv said "Way you made it before was perfect. Thanks. —I'm worried about his feet and walking to the restaurant," and Loretta said "You're not going to convince him to stay put here, so we'll do what he says. We'll walk slowly, or else put him in a cab, even for two blocks." "You think he'll let us pick up the check for once?" and she said "Fat chance. He's a Polish gentleman—that's what his friends called him—and no Polish gentleman ever let anyone else pick up the check or even split it." "What if there are two Polish gentlemen eating out together?" and she said "Do you always have to complicate it? But to answer, then after the desserts and teas had been ordered, he'd excuse himself to use the men's room and would grab the waiter when he was sure the other Polish gentleman couldn't see them, and pay the check then." "What if the other Polish gentleman used the same ruse but before him?" and she gave him a look: *Stop it, will you?* and he said "Okay, so long as you know I wanted to try." "Try all you like but let him win or you'll humiliate him, and then he won't eat out with us again." "Here we are," Hyman said, shuffling back with two glasses filled to the rim, spilling some from both and saying when Irv jumped up to get paper towels "Don't bother; I'll wipe it up later. The wine's for Loretta. Even if you said you didn't want any, this stuff is unbelievable. From the same client who also knows wine— goes for thirty dollars a bottle, he said—and I opened it just for you. You'll take the rest of it home with you. Go on, drink. It had to be a hard day for you, so you also need to relax."

Before that, they were on the Jersey Turnpike heading to New York. Loretta was in her wheelchair in back, earphones on, listening to a book on tape and occasionally dozing. *The Gulag Archipelago*, third volume. She'd finished the first two in a month. He was thinking of his visit to Leonard tomorrow. He'd once been in one of those places, twenty-five years ago. Went with Ron, a good friend, to see a bar acquaintance of theirs in a very expensive psychiatric ward on the East Side. The guy's parents were loaded and he checked himself in and out whenever he wanted. "There's So-and-So," he said in the recreation room, pointing to a soap opera actress Irv had never heard of but Ron had. "That glamourpuss over there is the daughter of the hottest apparels manufacturer in New York who's also the major benefactor of this spa. The very wing we're in and the coffee bar downstairs are named after the grandparents. Seated at the piano with his fingers splayed over the keys but never playing is the son of Such-and-Such… occasional novelist and well-known essayist of popular culture and frequent guest on late-night TV?—Come off it, you know who she is—you're a writer," and Irv said "What can I tell you?

I only read serious fiction and some French poetry and a bit of the classics and most likely the parts of the newspaper her name never gets in, and I don't watch TV." "Anyway, the son's a first-class fruitcake who'll never do anything in life but pass through here repeatedly. Lucky the family has oodles of money, though same could be said of me. But I have deep-seated interests and aims and the whatever-it-takes to bring them off. This time I'm really going to get started on making a feature-length documentary of my stay here." The place Leonard's at is altogether different. Tessie told him what to expect when he called for directions yesterday. Cross-Bronx Expressway, Major Deegan, and so on. Park in one of the visitor spaces in front. There are always plenty of spots, she said, since most of the patients don't get visitors, and the ones that do, the visitors usually don't have cars. "You'll go through security when you enter the building. Bring a photo ID with your signature on it, as they'll want to match your name and face and signature when you check in and out. A lot of the patients would like to escape. Once someone's admitted, he can't be discharged unless the medical team gives its okay or he's released to his family or another hospital. Don't be put off or unnerved by the twitchers and gibberers and crotch scratchers hanging out by the elevators. Some will look scary and a few might ask for and even demand money, cigarettes or drugs or pretend they can sell you some if you first turn over a few dollars, but they're all heavily medicated and harmless and would topple over with the puniest push of your pinky finger. Don't worry that they'll get on the elevator with you. The main floor is for the semi-insane, so they're all just rational enough to know that if they get off on another floor they might be forced to stay there. It's a lot different on Leonard's floor. That's why when you want to leave you'll have to punch a number code at the elevator, which one of the staff will give you. The main-floor patients are allowed to roam their dreary corridors freely. Some of the patients on Leonard's floor aren't even allowed out of their rooms except for meals and physical and psychotherapy sessions. When they are let out they're watched as closely as the overworked staff can, since the ratio of staff to patients is very low and the absentee rate and job turnover are high. And the filth and smells. The cleaning crew can only do so much. The poor souls, they work so hard for so little pay, but so many totally out-of-it patients pee and defecate on themselves or the floor or in bed and chairs before the aides can get them on a commode or slip a bed pan under them. It gets even worse than that. I've seen some of them masturbating in front of everyone or sticking their fingers in their anuses and tossing their feces around or intentionally upchucking meals minutes after they gorged themselves on them. Sometimes it's a cross between *Marat/Sade* and Bedlam without the paid audience and sadistic orderlies. It's odd how you start out feeling awful for the patients and after a few visits your heart goes out to the people taking care of them. None of them seem remotely mean or even sarcastic to the patients or cynical about their jobs. And Leonard, who's begun to bitch and crab about everyone including the kids and me and his dead parents, has never had a bad word about anyone working there. I am trying to find him a better-staffed and more cheerful-looking place and where his fellow immates aren't so crazy and crude, since it looks as if he'll need to be confined for the rest of his life. It isn't easy getting him into a place like that when you're doing it solely through Medicaid. The insurance plan we got, once his college one ended, doesn't cover such treatment, and I don't want to sell our house and then be left with nothing. We also haven't the means to pay for aides and equipment at home, and I'm not able to take care of him myself beyond the most minimal needs. Last few months at home he went beserk several times, and now his condition's much worse." "I remember," Irv said. "Once throwing you, or trying to, down the stairs. What can I bring him when I visit?" and she said "Box of chocolates. No, the other patients will quickly sniff out the goodies and start mooching them off you, and the box will be gone in five minutes. Just a blueberry muffin and 7-Up, which you'll have to protect, and which he likes more than anything and you can't get in the vending machines there." "Anything else I should know?" and she said "Maybe the directions again. It's easy to get lost once you get off Deegan and around the hospital, and that neighborhood isn't one you want to get out of your car in to ask for help. Another reason I'd like him to move. I want to feel safe in case my jalopy breaks down and the cell phone doesn't work."

So he goes, has brake trouble, drives around awhile till he finds a service station with a mechanic. The mechanic will only take cash. He doesn't have any, so the guy says "Then all the cash you have, and the rest with a check." "Oh God, let me see if I have one," and he does, tucked away in his wallet from about six months ago. Calls Loretta while the brakes are being fixed and says "How long you think you can hold out?" and she says "Maybe an hour more than we planned," and he says "Can you make it two? I've come this far, I really should see him." "Try and keep it short, then. If I have an accident, and I'm likely to, it'll mean a lot of cleaning up, which I hope you won't get angry at," and he says "I promise I won't; thanks." Finds the hospital fairly easily; he'd gone over the directions till he memorized them and also wrote them on a sheet of paper in big letters and taped it to the dashboard. Signs in at the entrance and shows his driver's license, and says "No thanks....Don't have any....I don't smoke....Sorry, just gave all my cash away to fix my brakes....This bag? It's for a friend here I'm visiting, and I don't want to open it, if you don't mind," as he makes his way down the corridor and waits for the elevator. Smells are as bad as Tessie said: shit, piss, vomit and something like Lysol. Gets off at the fourth floor and looks for the dining/recreation room; that's where she said Leonard will be. "After lunch, if he doesn't have to camp out on the toilet, they just leave him there for a couple of hours." He'll be in a chair that seems part eating table, part wheelchair; it has a tray on the front and wheels and handles on the back so it can be pushed. He'll have hightop sneakers on—huge sneakers; Leonard's a size 15, though he's only six feet tall. The laces will be untied and dragging on the floor. "Don't tie them," she said, "even if he asks. He's become too weak to walk—he only gets up to stand in his chair and stretch his legs a little—so he's not going to trip. For some reason—he must fool around with them—the laces always end up in double and triple knots when they're tied, and the aides often can't unknot them and twice they had to cut them off." Most likely he'll be sitting by himself, she said, no other person in any kind of chair within ten feet of him. "He must want it that way, and if any patient comes too close to him, I bet he tells them to shove off. I've never seen him do it, but I know when I'm not there lots of things happen I'm surprised at. For instance, and I've seen enough there to know it's more than possible, he talks about an ugly old woman, he calls her, who every few days, when nobody else is around, comes into his room and exposes her breasts and sometimes her genitals and makes suggestive tongue motions. I wonder if it hasn't gone even further than that. Leonard always had a lusty streak—chances are he still does, even with all the drugs—and it's obvious the woman is crazed. Though by the way he talks of her actions it seems he's repulsed by her." Leonard will be sleeping or

staring at something or still picking at his food, she said. He'll
be in sweats—"They're durable and cheap and easy for me to
wash and you don't have to iron them or futz around with
buttons and belts"—and have lost a lot of weight and some
head hair in front. She said she thinks that comes from one of
the medications he's taking, because he's also lost a considerable amount of body hair. "Leonard," Irv says, going up to him
after first approaching another patient in a chair he thought
was Leonard, both of them pale and gaunt from not going out
and just being sick, and that same loss of head hair, "how you
doing?" and Leonard looks up, without seeming to recognize
him, and then gives him a big smile and says "Hey, how are
you, how's it going, good to see you," and sticks out his hand
and Irv shakes it. "Thanks for coming, but you didn't have to,
you know. I'll be out of here before you leave yourself." "Very
good; your humor, it never flags," and Leonard says "Oh, I'm
a funny guy, all right. People always liked my jokes when I
cracked them. They also liked to crack my nuts, but that's a
story we won't go into. You're a funny guy too, always funny,
always cracking me up. But tell me, because I don't want to be
disrespectful to you or a fake, but what's your name again?
I know I know you and you're a funny guy who likes his wife
and kids, but it's names I'm not so good at today. Come back
tomorrow bright and early and I'll know what it is, even your
moniker, because tomorrow's not the day of the week I don't.
You're not Blondie, right? Dagwood? No. But don't make me

look bad by holding back what you know. Your name, come on, first, last and harmonica, give me your damn name," and looks angry and Irv says "Irv Dietz," and Leonard says "That's right, I didn't know it all the time," and smiles and says "Just kidding, and you thought I meant it before with that mean puss, but you'd be wrong. I didn't mean it what's so bit. Now what did I mean by that last, I'm serious? Come on, you're a smart guy, always was, always funny, you love your wife and kids, so it shows. People were always impressed with your smartness, and with me always knowing one of the smartest guys I know, so tell me what I said before or if I didn't," and he says "Now you're confusing me," and Leonard says "You're not confused, don't tell me. I'm confused, if there's anyone here, but you won't say that. Smart guys don't like opening their trap or getting like that. I don't know how they liked to get, and I won't pretend I do, because you're so smart you'll see me through, but they don't and you won't convince me any other ways. It's guys like this one and that one and everyone here one," pointing to patients and staff around the room, "who can't get out and are that way. She won't let me out," and he says "Who?" and Leonard says "You know who. Hey, what am I, a bird?—you-know-who, you-know-who. I'm not, and don't try to act stupid. Because you're smart, not stupid, and smart guys don't do stupid well. *She*. Who do you think? She's ruining my life." "Someone here? One of the nurses or aides?" and Leonard says "What did I tell you? Not one of them. Be smart and guess again." "If you mean Tessie—" and Leonard says "Yes, she, who else? Tessie. She's killing me keeping me here. She knows I want to go home. I told her; I got things to do there. I got my work. Children. I got a house. She's going to lose it because I'm not there to save it for her, and then we'll be none. I should call her. Got a nickel and a phone?" and he says "Leonard, phone calls cost a quarter now, maybe even fifty cents. They do in Baltimore from pay phones," and Leonard says "Who's talking about paying for the phones, and you're from Baltimore? I was once there. My brother went down and got lost and I was sent to visit him and bring him back. 'Anyway you can,' my father said, 'even if you have to strangle him.' But I couldn't find him. He was really lost, especially to me, because I was a good finder." "He was older. I remember you telling me," and Leonard says "Of course. Either older or younger but not the same age. It was that long ago, so I forget. I should call my father. Where is he? I want to see him. Why isn't he here too? He knows I need him," and Irv thinks his father's been dead a few years, died when he was close to a hundred, and says "Your father?" and Leonard says "Of course, what do you think I'm saying? Do I have to repeat every single phrase? You're supposed to be smart—I told you—not stupid. Pick up things easily; every little stick," and he says "I'm sorry. I'm a bit mixed up about some of the things you're saying. I don't know where your dad is either," and Leonard says "You don't, huh? That's because you don't know better. I know where he is. He's in there," and points over Irv's shoulder. Irv, who's sitting opposite him now in a regular chair, turns around to where Leonard's pointing and then back to him and says "Where? Who? What do you mean?" and Leonard says "I don't want to get into that." "Into what?" and Leonard says "That. That *what*. I don't play that game." "What game's that?" and Leonard says "There you go. That same game. I want to get out of here. I have to go home. You can't just say I can't. That shouldn't be it. That's not the game I play. See that man?" and he turns to where Leonard's pointing and sees an old man, a patient, sitting alone, eyes shut and jaw resting on his chest. "He's a great baseball player. He doesn't look it, but he's in great shape and I've seen him play. At the crack of the bat he can race from second to home in eight seconds flat. A record. Nobody else comes near to him, and with a perfect hook slide over the plate. He only stopped in here to catch his breath, which he does every day around now. Then he's back in the park, a kid running home." "You always liked baseball," and Leonard says "I liked to see and read it." "Did you read books on it when you were a kid? They were my favorites. *Homerun Hennesy* and others, and everything I could get on Jackie Robinson. I bet you did," and Leonard says "Sure. Everyone did when they were a kid. Hey, what do you think of my rhyme, yours and mine? There's another. We ought to team up as a team. That's no rhyme. But has there ever been one? That ever been done? Some stories I've read in lit magazines have been done by two, but not me and you. Only kidding with the last two." "They were good. One and done, two and you. You're sharp. The old Leonard. Though I know you never liked poetry much, you used to tell me. Just fiction," and Leonard says "And fiction about fiction and fiction writers. But I'm not the old Leonard. That was my old game. This place. It's no good for baseball or even reading about it. It was made for card players and gaming tables and kibbitzers. It smells of cigars and onions fried in butter and chicken livers. My mother would also hate it and be too critical. She gives me the jitters, so I don't want her here. Do something about it if I can't. If she comes in that door, which she said she would, I'm running the hell away. She messes up everything when she's not with my father. If he comes with her I'm throwing them both out the window. It's a long drop. I've seen people fall and heard the screams. I've never been to the Grand Canyon, but that's where they should go, straight to the bottom. You been there?" and he says "Loretta wants us to, but I tell her what am I going to see? Huge cliffs and deep gorges and a million other tourists. I'm not much for staring at nature. But you always said your mother was a nice quiet lady. Intelligent, very dignified, read a lot and encouraged your writing," and Leonard says "I don't know where you got that from, but it's one of your best fictions. She drove me mad when I was a kid, so leave her out of it. Though she can come if she wants. It's only between us two, her and me. If my father wants to be part of it, he's entitled to, for what he is in our family and all the bills he paid for years, but not you. I have to get out of here and home before she loses it," and he says "Who, your mother?" and Leonard says "How can you ask that question? My mother's not around; you know that. She died, ages ago, not when I was a baby, which is why I never talk about her. It's too sad to. My wife. I forget her name, that can happen to anyone, but my wife will lose our house." "You're worrying yourself over nothing, Leonard, really. I spoke to Tessie before I got here, and your home is absolutely safe. You're in no danger of losing it. It'll be there when you leave here, trust me." "You spoke to her?" and he says "For directions to get here. And then I called back to make sure, for I was afraid I'd get lost. I'm always getting lost when I'm trying to find an unfamiliar place in a neighborhood I've never been in," and Leonard says "Okay, I see the picture now. She won't come. You know that because she told you. She thinks if you come, she doesn't have to. She always says she will and she never does. One time she got lost coming here, something about a new neighborhood, and by the time she found it, it was dark, so she turned back. I told her that was a lie. I say please come every day, it's important for me. There are things I need done every day that only she can do. I say bring the kids and she says if they want to come they will, but she won't force them. I say come alone then and she says she will while they're in school, but do you see her here? Yesterday, today? Last week, last year?" "You haven't been here a year. In fact, it's been a relatively short time. Of course, no time's good, but you haven't been here as long as you say. And today's not a school day, so she probably couldn't get anyone to look after the kids and she couldn't phone you she wasn't coming because you have no phone." "She has her sister. We have friends. She could call someone in this place and send me a note. The office; they must have an office. But I'll be here for years, that's what I'm saying. I'll be forgotten, people will ask where I am, and no one will know I'm stuck here. She wants that so she can do what she wants with the house, lose it all," and he says "No, no, you're not making sense. Why would she want to lose the house? She wouldn't. And she still might come today," and Leonard says "Let her come tomorrow, or call the office with a note that she's on her way, because by then I'll be home, fixing up what she lost. I really have to get out of here. You get a chance to look around? It's no place to be. The accommodations are for a swine. If it was a hotel it'd go out of business. People keep me up all night. There are noises from six to six. The food's uneatable. The air's no good. The whole place stinks. You look outside to get away from it all and you see murderers and pushers on the street. So you stay away from the windows and all you get around you to look at are nut cases who could be murderers if you're dumb enough to turn your back on them. That's a big choice. They give you no choice. They put a dish of rotten food in front of you and say 'Eat, this is all there is,' and you want to throw up. You have to help me get my clothes. They put them somewhere, but you'll find them. Writers make good detectives. In my room, or maybe they got them in a locker. Not the rags I've got on but the ones I came in with and have to wear to get out. I can't leave in what I've got on. They'll spot me at the entrance and turn me back. They'll say 'Don't use the elevator, find your own way upstairs.' I'll say 'You know what's on the stairs. Murderers, addicts, pushers, crackpots, people who'll steal me blind.' They'll know I have a house, which nobody else here has, and they'll try to steal it, and the people who work here will be in with them." "Leonard, Leonard," putting his hand on Leonard's hand. "Let it rest a little, will you?" and Leonard pulls his hand away and says "What kind of expression's that. Say something I can understand. This is important. Right now I'm having a hard time too." "Okay, poorly worded, what I said. But your preoccupation about losing your house. That you think Tessie will, and all the other things that are worrying you, is all wrong and you should forget them." "*Are* all wrong. Speak English. You're a college teacher. Tessie and everything and losing *are* all wrong," and he says "Okay. But just relax, is what I'm saying. And that I might have made a mistake in grammar and with that 'let it rest a little' expression before and that you caught me on them? Good. Shows you're on top of things, using your mind well." "How can you say that? Do you take me for a fool? I don't fall for it. Don't think

I was born yesterday. Are all those all right as expressions? But you're a nice guy for coming. Nobody else has. Tessie says she will all the time, but she's never here. Look around. Do you see her? I don't have to look; I know she's not. I say to her 'Come every day. I need you to. A day passes and nobody like you has been here and it's night, I feel lousy.' My kids too. I have an older son out there. All right, the younger ones are young. I forget how old the older one is and his name, it's been so long. He's got to be big now, tall as you when you're standing, but he won't even come to deliver a newspaper to me. He could even be married and have kids but not a chauffeur. There could even be one named after me. That'd be a joke. His mother would kill him, so not so funny. She hates me the worst, but I used to love saying her name. 'Dearie, Dearie.' That isn't it, but early on it was close. All those people. Old friends and my folks. I don't want any of them here. See to that, will ya? They come, show them the door. Though it wouldn't hurt them if they tried," and Irv says "Let's change the subject for a minute. Here, I completely forgot. I bet you've been wondering what I've been holding in my lap. Good things come in little paper bags, so something I think you'll like," and opens the bag and puts a muffin and bottle of ginger ale on Leonard's tray. "What are those?" and he says "A blueberry muffin and ginger ale. Tessie said you'd like them. She said you'd like a 7-Up better, but the store didn't have it. When we were kids, every store carried 7-Ups." "That's true. You brought them for me? That's nice. Should I have them now?" "Tessie said if you don't have them right away, some of the other people here might want some, and then they'll be finished in no time flat. Maybe we should take a walk and find a quiet place if there's one and you can have them there," and Leonard says "You walk, I'll drive," and digs his heels into the floor and tries moving the chair forward that way, but isn't able to. "Maybe the brakes are locked," Irv says. "I've some familiarity with them with my wife's wheelchair," and checks and sees they're unlocked, and Leonard says "Even if it was the brakes, it won't go because it has no motor. You better drive." "You hold the soda and muffin, though," and gives them to Leonard and pushes him out of the room and down a hall and around the floor, but can't find a place where they can sit alone. "Which is your room? We can take the food there," and Leonard says "One of these doors. Mine has my name on it with some other guy's," and Irv finds it and they go there. He opens the soda and puts a straw in it—everything has to be drunk through a straw, Tessie said, or he can choke—and holds it up to Leonard's mouth and Leonard pushes it away. "I don't want it now. It's old, flat, the cake will crumble. Put them over there for later," and points to the dresser next to where Irv's sitting. Irv starts talking of old times. How they met: "Katya, remember her? And her name came quickly this time. Usually it takes a while for me to remember it. I don't know why. I lived with the woman for four years," and Leonard says "No, not even what she looked like. She's lost in the air. But she wasn't nice to you, was she?" "Oh no, she was nice. Funny, chipper, and very pretty and smart. I was probably more of a bastard to her than she was ever to me. Black hair? Big dark eyes? Not a full figure, but a good one, and kind of short? And as I said, she introduced us two," and Leonard says "That was good." Baseball: "I don't want to talk about the game," Leonard says. "Doesn't interest me anymore." "But before, didn't you say—" and Leonard says "Whatever I said, I don't know what's going on when I see it on TV, and too much noise. If you can't understand something from the beginning, put it down and pick up another book." A reading they gave together—"Actually, two, both of which I arranged. Jesus, I really went to bat for myself then, hawking my stupid stuff till I probably alienated half the literary world. Anyway, one at NYU, your alma mater, and the other at a bookstore on West Broadway." "That's true, my old school. I never liked it, and left before I graduated." "No, you did graduate. You and Suzanne at the same time." "That's good. Why go through all that if you can't get something out of it?" People they both know: "Why'd you bring him up?" Leonard says. "He's a shit. Hangs around because he thinks I can get his novel published. Once he knows I know nobody and can't even help myself and he gets published without me, he disappears. For do you see him here? He's a big man now, so he doesn't have to. Just like my parents and wife, for what's in it for them?" and Irv says

"Tessie comes a lot. Joseph, I know hasn't been here, but I'm sure he will. Probably doesn't think you're ready for visitors yet. You haven't been here long, so it's out of consideration for you." "You came," and he says "Well, hey, I know you for almost thirty years, so I got special rights." "That's true. I forgot. Thirty. You got a point." Someone else: "She's a fake," Leonard says. "Always was. If she sells you the moon, don't buy it. That's all I have to say about her. I've rubbed her out. Not a friend—out. None of those friends are friends—out. Let's talk about something else. I've gotten sour. I had nice pictures in my head before you started on them." Suzanne, his oldest son, Tessie. Leonard keeps shaking his head. "Nothing to say?" and Leonard says "I don't remember them, that's what." "You don't remember your first wife, and Manfred and Tessie?" and Leonard says "Okay, maybe her, the last one, but things come and go; you know that." "What about these? And just testing you; you don't have to answer," and gives the names of Leonard's two younger children. "Their names strike a bell?" and Leonard says "Talk about something else. I don't want to play this time." "The drive here? I had a little trouble; brakes. And I thought I'd get lost. But Tessie—your wife, if I can be a little bold to remind you—gave good directions," and Leonard says "Oh, she's bold, all right, and right out there. She's known for good directions. People call her if they want to go somewhere and they don't know, and she's never gotten anyone lost. That's how she makes her living, giving directions by phone. You want to get home, call her and she'll tell you, right to your front door and no traffic along the way even during rush hour. Because we know you, you won't have to pay. You come by car or train?" and he says "Car." "That's good. It's fast and sound. Trains are good too, but you got to walk after. My kids and I are lucky. What are those?" pointing to the top of the dresser, and Irv says "The photos of your little kids?" "No." "The bottle of soda and paper bag?" and Leonard says "Yeah, what are they?" "Ginger ale and a blueberry muffin inside the bag. I brought them for you. You said you didn't want them yet and to put them there. I wanted to get you a 7-Up...anyway, want them now?" and Leonard says "No, you didn't." "Yes, I told you this before. The store didn't have 7-Up—" and Leonard says "She put them there. I told her not to. Explicitly: don't. She heard me. She's not deaf. People are always pretending not to hear, you notice that? But that's the only thing that isn't wrong with her." "Who?" and Leonard says "Don't do that. Please don't say 'who?' We've gone over this. You know who. I don't know why you're still doing it, unless to annoy me," and he says "Honestly, I don't know. I'm sure I could guess whom the person you're speaking about is, but if I started guessing I bet you'd tell me not to play that kind of game." "There, you're doing it again. I say don't say 'who,' and you say 'whom,' but they're the same thing, and you're using it wrong. Don't play that game either. The game you just played. It really annoys me why people can't listen, even those who are supposed to be bright. Don't. Do me a favor. Be a friend. I told you not to. My mother. It's obvious she put them there," and he says "When do you think she did that?" "What's the difference when? She did it. It's done. She's always doing things like that. She plays the game better than anyone. You know her, so you know. Is and always. Move them away, please?" and he says "If you're not going to eat and drink them, want me to throw them out?" and Leonard says "Just get them out of my sight." Irv puts them behind the framed photos of Leonard's young children and says "You know, you say I knew your mother, but I never met her. I remember, you'd come to the city and we'd have lunch and then you'd often go downtown to see your parents—they were on Park Avenue South by then—and, eventually, only your father. You met my mother a few times. I'm not saying anything's peculiar about this: you met, I didn't, etcetera. But sometimes we'd take walks down Broadway, stopping in a couple of bookstores and having coffee someplace, and end up at my mother's apartment and usually have a drink with her. Or I'd have a drink with her and you'd have juice or a glass of water. You didn't drink alcohol. Probably still don't, right, not even wine or beer?" and Leonard says "I never liked it of any kind. Didn't taste good and a small bit of it made me dizzy and edgy. I didn't want to be that. I thought I had to have my head. I also saw your mother at your wedding. We talked. That was a grand affair, a terrific feast. Waiters there, right?" and he says "No,

buffet. We laid all the food out on a long table and the champagne and wine on another, and people helped themselves."
"But not your father there. He must've been dead." "That's
right; just a few months before I met you. Good, though, how
you remember the wedding. One of the coldest January days
on record in New York, the newspaper said. Five below. The
windows of our apartment... both the ceremony and reception
took place in it," and Leonard says "I remember. Cold." "We'd
had the windows cleaned the day before by a professional
window cleaner, and they were covered with ice the next day
because of all the breathing going on inside. I'm sorry, did that
make sense?" and Leonard says "Sure, sense. Dollars and
cents and *mucho dinero*. That wedding cost a small fortune.
Had to, and it was very cold." "My brother drove you back to
the Port Authority bus terminal uptown, remember that? It
was so cold out, his car wouldn't start, so you and I pushed it
for about fifteen minutes till we got it going," and Leonard
says "Those things I don't remember. But I do your mother
and also what she was wearing." "What was she?" and Leonard
says "Clothes," and smiles. "Ah, you got me with a good one,"
and Leonard says "I try. But my mother, we've talked about
her, so we don't have to anymore. But she comes in, and she
will—that's the kind of thing she'd do; just charge in and take
over—tell her not to. If she insists but promises to be on her
best behavior, okay, because then she acts good for a while.
But not my father. Oh no, not that guy. I don't want him here

at any cost. He upsets me too much. Makes me dizzy and then my head goes astray," and he says "But you always said you liked your father. I never met him, but he seemed like a nice sweet guy. Your mother? From everything you've said and written about her, she was a little, well, not altogether there at times, we'll say, which must have been rough on you, but also very kind," and Leonard says "So you do know her, you see? Why'd you ask about her, then, to try and fool me? Games. Everyone's full of them, but all right. And my father was all right too, but I don't want either of them here. They come, they'll change everything. If you have rugs on the floor, they'll hang them on the walls. Bare bones become fat with them, and they drive like cowboys. After that, they'll want to stay here. I want to get out. You see the problem. Out, in. It's all been reversed. The room's too small for us all. But they know how to get their way, so you can be sure they'll stay. The parents who came to dinner. That was a funny show. Let me have that, what I didn't before," and points to the framed photos on the dresser. "You want these?" Irv says, taking the muffin out of the bag and holding it up with the soda, and Leonard says "No, why would you think I would? Junk them. And whatever it is with them, the flowers. She put them there and she shouldn't have and she knows it. I told you not to let her, you did, okay, it's done, why sweat over it?" "So you want me to junk the muffin and soda and put the flowers someplace where you can't see them? If it's something you think you're allergic to,

they're not real, you know." "Good, because I can't smell anything anyway, which is a good thing here. Now there's a good
line," and Irv says "It was good; You're really cooking today
with those lines," and Leonard says "Cooking with gas, we
used to say, before everything became electric. Our kitchen is,
every appliance now, though she's going to lose it along with
the house. But use the line. And the one I just made. Use
everything. I can't anymore, you see that, so take it all. You're
good at that," and he says "What, taking? Your material? When
did I ever?" "I didn't say that. I don't know what I said, but not
that. You're a good guy; it's me who can't work anymore, that's
all I meant. I once did it pretty good. So-so to pretty good, I can
honestly say that. Nobody else will, honestly or dishonestly, so
I'll say it myself. Never great. I would never say great, and
even if I once was I would never say it. But I wasn't, that's all
there is to it, but I was never that bad either. I was once okay,
I'll say. I'll settle on that, wouldn't you? But you can have all
the lines. I've no place to put them, for one thing. For another,
I don't know. So I have to give them up. Everything's gone
wrong. You see that. What happened to my life? A lousy line,
but what has to be said. I'm a mess. I'm in a stinking place. I'm
surrounded by bad food and hooligans. I used to have a house
and clean clothes and now I got to get out of here to save it,"
and he says "You still have your house. I told you: I spoke to
Tessie yesterday and she's all right and says the house is too
and so are your kids and you shouldn't worry about anything."

"What kids are those?" and he says "Your two from Tessie. You remember their names?" and Leonard says "Sure I do but I forget them now. What are they?" and he gives them and Leonard says "They don't sound like mine. She was always fooling me," and he says "Tessie? No," and Leonard says "Of course, Tessie, who else? You're playing those games with me again. The more I'm here, the more you play them and everyone else. Like the guy running past the door," and Irv turns to look. "He's not there anymore; he's too fast. A ballplayer, another great one, but someone who plays these other kinds of games too. I guess you're good at one, you're good at the others. A natural athlete, you can say, which I bet you were too, the easy way you do things, so not just you. You're all right. But whatever you say, I have to get out of here; it's a must," and he tries standing up in his chair as if he wants to get out of it, and Irv says "Sit, Leonard, sit. You can fall and hurt yourself," and Leonard says "You think so? Okay; you know," and sits and points to the top of the dresser and says "What's that doing there? She moved it again. It was once another place, somewhere it should have been, but now it's here where it doesn't belong," and Irv says "Which one you mean?" and Leonard says "Don't start again. The vase. You knew that. And those things that go in it, but if I just say vase, you'll know. She moved it. I don't want her here. She comes in when I'm not around and rearranges everything. The bed, furniture, what's on top of them, and he'll go along with everything she does.

Though she wasn't all bad. I don't want you to think that. I had a pretty good life as a kid. I got a lot. They didn't stint. I once had a brother. She didn't play ball with me but the other guy did. I never saw him. I haven't in years." "Your father? Brother?" and Leonard says "Who do you think? My father. My brother's who I wanted to play ball with. He was always at work," and he says "Your father manufactured shoelaces, didn't he? Had a small factory in Brooklyn or Queens, you once said," and Leonard says "I never knew what he did. It could be what you say. He was a mystery. Went off in the light and came back in the dark, except on Fridays. He never spoke of it, read his Jewish newspaper under a dim bulb, hardly acknowledged me, but I always had new shoelaces and lots of laces of different sizes and colors to give away to schoolmates I wanted to be my friends. They liked the sneaker laces best. He once made some that were chartreuse and fuchsia and shocking pink. My mother wouldn't let me wear them—too loud—but every kid in every borough did and for a while we were rich. Now they'll both come here and say 'How could this have happened? We always knew you'd come to this. Get up, get your clothes on, don't pretend to be sick. Get your big carcass out of here,'" and he says "That's what they used to say to you as a kid?" and Leonard says "No, I'm just talking to you. He also made shoehorns and shoetrees and shoepolish, but they never did as well as the laces and they blamed it on me. How come you came?" "You mean here, today?" and Leonard says "I don't know what I mean, because what did I say?" and he says "The truth is, I don't know why I thought your question needed elucidating. It was clear enough and my question to it only confused things. To see you, that's why I came. You're my old friend and I wanted to see how you were." "How am I? Did you find out and can you tell me?" "You're fine. A little dissatisfied and agitated with your lot here, but that's natural—I'd be too. I'll speak to Tessie about it, see what we can do to change and improve things for you. I just wish I could come here more often and stay longer. But my wife is home alone and I can't, and I'm only in New York about once a month." "If I'm so fine and you see me how I am, how come you won't help me get out of here? What kind of friend is that? You come here, you leave, you drink your coffee, but you won't help me? They will. They'll say it's a shame and a pity I'm here and a family disgrace to be in such a place and it costs too much besides. And I'm losing my house in the bargain, they'll say, and then where will they stay when they visit me, so they have to get me out of here right away. They'll do that, so why not you while you have the time? You're better and bigger built and not as old." "I wouldn't be allowed. I'm just a friend. I don't have the authority to check you out of here and I wouldn't know where to take you if I did." "To my home, where do you think? You have my permission, to hell with the rest. You're strong and can also talk your way through, so the hell with everyone who won't help me—just push them out of the way. Stiff-arm them, that was

the word. Or straight-arm them—football, not my sport.
Parents always stick up for their kids, so mine will if you won't.
They'll drive like cowboys, so who knows if we'll get there,
but it'll still be a lot better than this. My lot will be better. I'm
tired of baseball and never liked football—too dumb and
rough. There's too many ballplayers here as it is and they're all
much better players than me. They have pros here from every
big team. They can play all they want together, have a snack,
and go. My father was good too. A real smart operator. Fast on
his feet in shoes—he didn't need sneakers—and with huge
muscles in his neck, so he'll help me more than anybody. Then
I'll be free of this dive. Because here—you see it; you have a
wife and home—but my life is over. You're a smart operator
also, so maybe that's the way. I don't belong here. It's all day,
it's all night. I go no place, so I never come back. My head's
twisting in riches but I've got glue up to my nose. When I ask
to go, they won't let me. When I don't want to go, they say to
get lost and make me sit in my own stew. Is that a way to go? I
got to get my good clothes on. Not for my own funeral, but to
leave the other way. In those, they won't see me. Then my
folks can drive up and take me to my home. I should marry
again, become my own father. That'd be the thing to do if he
doesn't come. I should get a good clean wife like yours, even
if she is ill, who'll look after me till I'm on my own. Tell them
to get lost when they're not nice to me or say they can't. You
can do that. Flex your neck muscles and scare them away."

"Who do you want scared away, someone on the staff?" and Leonard says "The party of the worst sort who boss everyone around. Tell them I'm you're old friend whose house you want to save. That there could even be a fire started and we've got to leave to put it away." "Much as I'd like to, I can't do anything like that. But if you're saying you're being mistreated here—" and Leonard says "I'm saying a lot of things. Some of them make sense. Call my parents then, if you can't help me, because they won't let me touch a phone. They say it's a quarter now from a booth and I've no loose change. I haven't seen them for so long that I now think they should come. If they don't, and this is the sad news, no one else will help me get out of here, so call them for me, okay? You know their number. I told you to carry it on you at all times just in case. For if I'm not out of here fast, I'll die from going nuts. Tell them that too. Be ruthless. They tell you they're sick or busy or on vacation or too old, tell them you know better than that. This place is full of crazies, you should say, so not the ideal spot for their son. Bluh bluh bluh. You laugh, but I'm not kidding you. It sounds funny coming from me, but there's a woman here who does that all the time. She's just for instance but is maybe the worst for me. Stands outside my room when she knows I don't want her to and what it does to me, and bluh-bluhs me blue in the face. I want to kill her. Get a hit man if not me. Not that but knock her down and disorder her gums so she can't bluh-

bluh me anymore or at least to give it a rest. I want to sleep and think and daydream of other days, but she won't let me. To conceive of strategies to flee from here, but I can't when she's bluh-bluhing interminably. Every day and twice on Sundays: tell them to chase her away. All of them. One's worse than the other. Outside my room they're the worst. In here when you're with me and the room's otherwise empty, they can't get me as bad. But they'll hang outside it waiting for you to leave; then they'll pounce. Turn around—go on, you'll see them," and Irv turns around to the door, nobody's by it, and says "I'll close the door if you want," and Leonard slaps his forehead and says "Why didn't I think of that? No brains, or little left; you're the only smart guy now. All these times I could have just slammed it in their faces. Sure, do it; we can talk better that way," and Irv starts for the door and Leonard says "No, it's *verboten*. They'll think 'What's going on in there?' and then the punks who run this joint will get even with me, more stew. So keep it open. If it's closed they won't be able to find me when dinner rolls roll around. But what do I care about dinner? I can't eat. The food's *drek*. I can't sleep. The whole place is in trouble. I don't know how I got myself into such a jam, but I have to get out. You got to help me. Not just with words, for if it's not you, what is there? My wife and folks, and you know as well as me how hard it is to get them here and then for them to do anything. Eventually they would, one or the other, but that could take days. So get me dressed, will you? Not to put my clothes on—just give me them. Over there, or in there, or somewhere," his hand pointing jerkily around the room, "but get me some of the street ones, even if they're not clean." Irv says "Listen, I don't want to leave you like this. I'll stay till you calm down. But I have to go. My wife, Loretta—you know; she's home alone. I couldn't get anyone to look after her and then I spent almost two hours getting the brakes fixed coming here, and I don't want to leave her too long. I can't. Accidents can happen. A year ago she broke her nose in one, right in our apartment here. Fell out of her wheelchair, even though she was strapped in. I don't know how she did it. She must have leaned forward too far and the whole chair fell over. I was there at the time too, writing in the next room. I heard the crash and ran in and saw she had smashed her face on the coffee table. I had to take her to Emergency at St. Luke's. I wheeled her there—it was only a few blocks—because I didn't want to hang around for an ambulance, and they made us wait an hour and I had to stop the bleeding there myself with paper towels. We also have to start back to Baltimore in an hour or so and there are lots of things I have to do for her before we go. If we don't leave by four it'll mean I'll have to drive the last hour or two in the dark, and my eyes aren't good for that anymore," and Leonard looks angry and says "You guys are always leaving. Flit in, flip out, but go. Just when things were going good and we're talking and having laughs about what idiots we once were, and you came to see me, right, and not some bag lady? For how long you been here, five minutes, ten?" and he says "It's been more than an hour. There's also the half hour or more it'll take to get back to the apartment if I don't get lost, and then finding a parking spot, which shouldn't be too tough now on a Sunday. I told you—she can't be left alone too long, and four hours, which is what it'll come to, is over the max," and Leonard says "Sure, I remember. It's a damn shame for her. Such a sweet woman, and so brainy, and to get so sick. Give her my best, will you? Think she remembers me? It seems so long, and from my wife too; everybody. Say hello and that we're thinking of her. And thanks for coming. I hope you don't mind if I don't walk you to the door," and grins. Irv says "That was a good one," and wants to kiss his cheek but knows he doesn't like that between men—he said it a couple of times before he got sick: "Guys shake hands and pat backs; what's with this kissing business?" "I should probably wheel you back to the main room," and Leonard says "Nah, I'll nap. Out there it's too much commotion for it. Nurses'll know where I am when they want me." "Need anything before I go? Feet raised, glass of water?" and Leonard says "I'm fine." "And the soda and muffin. You want to save them for later?" and Leonard says "Dump them." Irv puts them in the trash can in the room's bathroom, shuts the door, pees, comes out and pats Leonard's shoulder and says "See you soon, huh?" and Leonard says "Good," and he leaves. He goes to the elevator, presses the button and waits for more than a minute and presses it again and keeps pressing. "Oh God, I forgot," he says, and sees an aide passing and says "What's the number code of this keypad, I think you call it, to get the elevator?" and she gives it and he presses it and in a few seconds the elevator comes.

Stephen Dixon is the author of 23 books of fiction, including the National Book Award–nominated novels *Frog* and *Interstate*. His short fiction has won most of the major literary awards, including an O. Henry Award and a Pushcart Prize, and he is the recipient of honors from the Guggenheim Foundation, the National Endowment for the Arts, and the American Academy of Arts and Letters. He is on the faculty of Johns Hopkins University.